POTIONS & PAPERBACKS

A LIBRARY WITCH MYSTERY

ELLE ADAMS

This book was written, produced and edited in the UK, where some spelling, grammar and word usage will vary from US English.

To be notified when Elle Adams's next book is released, sign up to her author newsletter.

1

"Never poke a sleeping vampire with a stick."

I stared at the first sentence I'd written for a long moment before striking through the words with my pen. They were fine, just... lacking something. "Aunt Candace never told me starting a book was this difficult."

"What is that?" Cass walked up behind me. "That's not your dad's journal, is it?"

"No." I swiftly closed the notebook, but my cousin had already read the scratched-out words over my shoulder.

"Poke a vampire with a stick?" she asked. "Never a good idea, but your friend Laney might let you poke her without decapitating you. Evangeline, though? Not a chance."

I made a noncommittal noise, but it didn't deter her.

Cass peered over my shoulder. "You're not talking about actually poking a vampire," she observed. "What're you writing?"

"Nothing." I shrugged, a flush creeping up my neck. "I just figured I ought to take notes for the next unsuspecting person who might need them."

"You're writing your own journal?" At my cousin's words,

I tensed, but her expression showed no hint of mockery. "You're not writing it in code?"

"Definitely not," I said firmly. "Dad meant well, but I don't know if he expected it to take months or years for me to decipher all his journal entries."

He'd been worried about his words falling into the wrong hands, which was fair; many extremely dangerous people had wanted their hands on that journal and had gone as far as to threaten my life to get it. If I followed in his footsteps, my own journal would likely end up inspiring similar behaviour, but as long as I didn't take it outside of the library like my dad took his, I'd theoretically be fine to risk writing it in plain English rather than an elaborate code I'd made up that nobody else knew.

I'd been working on my dad's journal for months, and while I'd already extracted the most useful pieces of information, my chaotic life at the library left little time for painstaking side projects. My aunt Adelaide was currently up to her neck in the year's taxes, leaving me to watch the front desk, but even the lack of new visitors to the library didn't stop the constant interruptions. When my cousin departed, my familiar, Jet, fluttered down and landed on the desk.

The little crow peered at the notebook, eyes bright and intrigued. "Are you writing a story?"

"No, and please don't tell Aunt Candace," I muttered to him. "We don't need her asking questions—"

"Don't tell me what?" My aunt appeared from behind a bookcase, as if summoned by my words. *Typical.*

"What're you doing downstairs?" My aunt wore the jumbled clothing she usually did on a deadline—a flowery red dress with pink leggings that clashed horribly with her red hair—and was accompanied by the usual pen and notebook floating at her side. I knew, however, that it wasn't a normal deadline that held her attention.

"Taking a walk, and don't change the subject," she said. "What exactly are you writing?"

"Nothing now." I picked up the notebook and slipped it into my pocket. "I was going to start a list to keep track of what I'm reading. That's all."

"Why use a list when you can just start a dozen books at once and never finish any of them?" She laughed, her notebook and pen bobbing up and down next to her. "No, I don't think you're being quite truthful."

"Aunt Candace, stop bothering Rory." Estelle approached the desk, carrying a stack of books, which she deposited in the returns box. "Care to help me put these back where they belong? The students decided to leave them lying around instead of returning them to their shelves."

"No thanks." Aunt Candace sidestepped the desk. "I have a mystery to solve."

She vanished amid the shelves in a swirl of red hair, her notebook and pen flying in pursuit.

Estelle bent over the box, red curls bouncing around her round, friendly face. "Can you help me with these, Rory?"'

"Of course." At times like these, I understood why Aunt Candace often locked herself in her room upstairs for days at a time when she needed to finish a book. I'd have no chance of getting anything written down at this rate.

I got up and helped Estelle return the books to their correct shelves, wishing the students would clean up after themselves for once. Since it was the start of the new school year, we had fewer summer school attendees showing up for various activities throughout the day, but that didn't stop the undergraduates from Ivory Beach's only university from coming in at all hours and leaving a mess behind them. Luckily, most of the books had come from the ground floor, which contained the reference area as well as the fiction section. Upstairs were more specialised areas, covering three floors—or four, if you counted the newly rediscovered fourth-floor corridor—and including some of the library's more dangerous inhabitants.

When I'd first met my late father's estranged family just under a year ago, I'd never have guessed that their magical library would become my home. Nor would I have guessed how familiar I'd become with its towering stacks and hidden alcoves—though parts of it always remained hidden to me. From trapdoors hiding sleeping vampires to shelves that moved where they pleased, the library contained a seemingly infinite number of secrets, and the rediscovered fourth-floor corridor that had vanished years ago was only the most recent of them.

"If Aunt Candace spends much more time upstairs, she'll end up missing her deadline," I told Estelle as we returned a stack of yellowing manuscripts to a cabinet inside one of the private rooms off the lobby. "If she hasn't already. I know there's not much we can do when she gets like this, but I don't really want her legions of angry fans to show up on the doorstep if she doesn't put out a new title soon."

"You know Aunt Candace. She can only have one obsession at a time." Estelle closed the cabinet door on the manuscripts. "I can guarantee she'll get bored eventually and go back to her books. She hasn't made any progress on opening those doors."

"True." I followed Estelle out of the room and returned to the front desk, where we found Jet chattering away to the library's resident pixie, Spark. I suspected Spark didn't understand much English and was just being polite, but Jet didn't get to gather as much gossip for Aunt Candace now that her fixation was on the upstairs corridor instead.

"Where's Sylvester?" I asked. "I haven't seen him in a while."

"Haven't a clue." Estelle tipped out the last couple of books from the returns box. "Probably napping."

"Or spying on Aunt Candace." The owl had taken the existence of the fourth floor as a personal insult, since it was the only part of the library outside of the vast realm of his knowledge, and he refused to get involved directly. He would still be watching the situation from afar, however.

As a genius loci, or the animal-shaped embodiment of the library itself, Sylvester prided himself on being privy to all of its secrets and had gone into a tremendous sulk when the corridor had reappeared after decades of being hidden even from the owl's watchful eyes. Therefore, he'd even stopped hanging out with Cass, Estelle's younger sister, who spent most of her time on the third floor with her dangerous magical pets.

"Is it just me, or is it quieter than usual down here?" I said while helping Estelle carry the three remaining books to the reference area. "I know everyone went back to school this week, but the library isn't normally this calm."

"That means someone's about to cause trouble, in my experience." Estelle pushed one book into place on its shelf, and I did the same to my own. "Like Cass is going to adopt a new pet, or Aunt Candace is going to lose her memory again."

"I bet on the latter." Temporarily losing her memory hadn't been enough to deter my aunt from probing the depths of the fourth-floor corridor in the hopes of unearthing its secrets. "Or Evangeline's about to show up and want a tour of the corridor."

"I hope not." Estelle shuddered. "Why would she be interested in what's up there?"

"She's a vampire. Knowledge and secrets are to her what dangerous magical monsters are to Cass."

Vampires prided themselves on knowledge, and Evangeline was no exception. She'd taken more than a passing interest in my dad's journal, given his previous entanglements with the dangerous group known as the Founders, but my grandmother's secret corridor had yet to capture her attention.

Granted, the corridor was mostly empty, but that was because nobody could figure out how to get through any of the doors. The library's keys didn't work on the locks, and my grandmother had left no maps or other clues for us to follow. Although we'd managed to get the guardian of the corridor to stop cursing anyone who set foot in there, that didn't mean we'd figured out how to crack its secrets—though that didn't stop Aunt Candace's relentless efforts.

"They've been quiet lately too," Estelle said. "The vampires."

"Yeah." I might have worried about tempting fate by mentioning them, but rarely had I gone through this long a stretch of time without seeing one of the fanged locals. "Not counting Laney, of course."

My best friend was Ivory Beach's newest vampire, turned by one of the Founders—the vampires who'd wanted my dad's journal and had been prepared to commit murder to get it. Unfortunately, I wasn't the only person they'd targeted, and by the time I'd realised the extent of their network, it'd been too late to stop my best friend from suffering permanent consequences. Luckily for everyone involved, she was having the time of her life being one of the undead. Or should that be time of her *after*life?

"Of course, but she's not one of *them,*" Estelle said. "Has she mentioned Evangeline recently?"

"Aside from her habit of swooping around being terrifying?" I wasn't entirely sure how most vampires spent their endless days except by playing mind games and trying to outwit one another. "No, and she didn't bring up the Founders either."

"You haven't heard from her since the note... right?"

"Nope." The Founders had delivered me an ominous note on behalf of Mortimer Vale, their leader, who was currently incarcerated in one of the magical world's most high-security prisons. He'd implied that spies for the Founders hid within Ivory Beach itself, and when I'd very reluctantly told Evangeline about the note, she'd responded by going ominously quiet.

Since then, we'd caught one of Mortimer Vale's human contacts, Lisa Grubbins, and while I'd been inclined to think Lisa herself had left the note, she'd lost all memory of the library thanks to her own meddling and had likely forgotten the Founders too. For that reason, we had yet to find out if she'd been working alone.

"I found it!" Aunt Candace marched into view wearing a triumphant expression, as if we were supposed to have a clue what she was talking about.

"Found what?" said Estelle.

"A clue, of course." She waved a piece of paper in the air. "I've been testing different revealing potions and spells on all those closed doors up on the fourth floor, and I finally found one that worked."

"What's that, then?" The piece of paper didn't look remarkable to me. "Was it behind the door?"

"No, the door didn't open," she said. "But it *did* show me some very interesting text. Look at this."

She thrust the paper in front of my nose. After scrutinizing her illegible handwriting for several moments to decipher the words beneath, what I saw made my heart skip a beat, and Estelle let out a startled gasp.

The words were written in the same code as my dad's journal.

"What... those were written on the door?" Estelle raised her head to look at our aunt.

My mouth parted. "Did my grandmother know the code?"

"Apparently so." Aunt Candace's excitable tone suggested this information was going straight into her next book. "Well?"

"'Well' what?" Did she want my opinion? Or... "If you want me to fetch the translation spell, there's no harm in asking nicely."

"It was my spell, remember?" she said. "Besides, I thought you might be interested to know how and when your father and grandmother shared that code."

I did, but if I handed the translation spell over to my aunt, there were no guarantees I'd get it back anytime soon. However, she'd piqued my curiosity. "Fine."

"I'll tell my mum," Estelle offered. "You'll watch the desk in the meantime, won't you, Aunt Candace?"

Aunt Candace gave a world-weary sigh. "I *suppose.*"

The spell was upstairs in my room, and fetching it wouldn't take more than two minutes, but I decided against pointing that out. Estelle shot me a sympathetic look over her shoulder as she proceeded to the back room, while I headed into the small corridor off the lobby that led to our family's living quarters. I climbed the narrow staircase one floor up and entered my room, where I grabbed the box-shaped spell I'd left on my bedside table. My aunt had crafted the spell to help me crack the code in which my dad had written years of diary entries, but I'd thought the code was one he'd made up himself. Apparently, though, Grandma had known it too.

Strange. Why hide the truth from her own family? My dad had moved outside of the magical world when he'd married my mother, and discussing magic with normals was strictly forbidden. But Grandma had always lived in the library and would have no need to keep the code hidden.

I returned downstairs with the spell and handed it to Aunt Candace. She placed the box upon the desk and pushed the piece of paper into the letterbox-style slot in the side while Estelle and I watched warily nearby.

"My mum told you not to take any dangerous risks," Estelle informed Aunt Candace.

"Too late." Aunt Candace watched the box reverently. "Let's see what this says..."

A few moments later, the page emerged from the box. So did a second sheet of paper upon which several words were printed. "What language is that?" I asked.

Aunt Candace snatched up the new page. "Another code. How intriguing."

"It translated the code into another one?" Estelle asked. "Why would it do that?"

"Because my mother loved a good enigma." Aunt Candace grinned as if all her birthdays and Christmases had come at once. "Excellent."

"That's one way of putting it." I exchanged a baffled look with Estelle and then swivelled to my aunt when she tucked the box under her arm and began to retreat. "Hey! Where are you going with that?"

"To try some experiments," she answered. "You don't still need it for your dad's journal, do you? You'll be in the grave before you finish, at this rate."

"That's because people keep interrupting me."

She gave another laugh. "Well, if I let people's interruptions deter me, I'd never finish a book. Fear not, Rory—I'll return this to you in one piece."

She vanished among the shelves, presumably to one of the classrooms at the back, where she could test her most hair-raising spells without affecting the rest of the library.

"Great." I stifled a sigh. "Shouldn't she look up the second code before she starts casting spells on the box?"

"Not if it'll just turn into a third one." Estelle's brow furrowed. "If I had to guess, the spell must be woven into the very words themselves. Our grandmother must have been determined that nobody get through that door."

"Why, though?" That was what I didn't understand. "We're her family. And the corridor itself is inaccessible to anyone who isn't one of us."

"I wish I knew." She pursed her lips. "A lot of the chaos she left behind was because she didn't expect to die. Maybe she did intend to show us the corridor herself someday."

"Along with the map of the library that doesn't exist," I added. "What do we do now, then? I'm not sure Aunt Candace's bull-in-a-china-shop approach is going to crack that code. She's more likely to set the box on fire."

"True. I wonder…" Estelle trailed off. "I know at least one professor at the academy who might know. He's an expert on code spells and the like."

"Really?" She hadn't mentioned that when I'd been working on my dad's journal, but once I'd got hold of the document in which my dad had laid out the code, the translator spell had been sufficient for me to render the journal in plain English.

"I figured you didn't want any strangers getting involved when you were struggling with your dad's journal," she clarified. "This, though… it's not just a code. It's another kind of spell altogether."

"A spell that causes the text to evade translation spells?" I surmised. "The actual words are bewitched? How is that possible?"

"I'd like to know the same." Estelle pulled out her phone. "I'll message Professor Booker and see what he thinks. I'm sure this isn't news to him—I remember he once told me a story about a translation that melted the eyeballs of anyone who tried to read it."

"What?" I raised a brow. "Is Aunt Candace aware that might be a possibility?"

"Yes, but she won't let a bit of mild peril get in her way."

"She needs her eyeballs to read. You'd think she'd be more careful."

A rap on the front door made us both jump, then I relaxed; only one person was polite enough to knock before entering. Xavier, my boyfriend and the local Grim Reaper's current apprentice.

When I called "Come in," Xavier entered the library, looking no more dead than I was. Blond curls framed his face, and his eyes were a deep shade of aquamarine.

"Hey, Rory," he said. "Is this a bad time?"

"No—it's fine," I said. "Just, you know. Aunt Candace."

"You two can go for a walk and talk about it," Estelle said to us. "It's quiet enough in here that I can watch the desk myself."

"If you're sure." I didn't mind getting some air, though my lunch break wasn't for another hour or so. "I'll see you in a bit. If Aunt Candace sets anything on fire, let me know, okay?"

Xavier and I left the library hand in hand, walking out into the cool sea air. The square was as empty as the library, with only a handful of people venturing into the shops and bakeries.

"I guess tourist season is over." I shivered a little in the brisk wind. The sun was hidden behind a mass of clouds in the overcast sky. "How's your boss?"

"As sociable as a vampire in the daytime," he replied. "So, the usual. What's going on with your aunt?"

"A new development in the fourth-floor corridor," I said. "My grandmother outdid herself on security measures."

"Not another guardian monster, I hope?"

"Nah. Aunt Candace was trying to open one of the doors, and she managed to get it to reveal some text, but it's... well, it was written in the same code as my dad's journal."

His brows shot up. "Did you translate it?"

"We tried, but the words turned into another code instead."

"That's inconvenient." He paused for a moment while we walked past a harried-looking witch with a pushchair containing twin girls who appeared to be engaged in a duel with a pair of fake wands. Their shrieks echoed in the background as we continued towards the seafront, where the scents of ice cream and sand mingled in the cool breeze.

"Pretty much," I said in response to Xavier. "Aunt Candace ran off with the translation spell to try some experiments, which means I won't see it for at least a week."

"That's not fair of her," he commented. "Especially since it didn't actually work."

"I know." I faced the turbulent waters of the ocean, as if the sight of the waves lapping against the sand would wash away the uncertainty in my mind. "She also implied I was being too slow to translate my dad's journal."

"It's a big job, and you're busy, right?" he said. "Besides, you've made good progress."

"Yeah... I do wish he'd written a version in plain English, though." I shook my head. "Though my grandmother might be worse. I've never heard of a spell that makes a text impossible to read, at least, not by someone who actually wanted someone to be able to read it."

"I imagine she did it for a good reason. Did Estelle have any ideas?"

"Estelle said one of her professors at the university might be able to help, but who knows," I said. "It's not urgent by any means, but you know how Aunt Candace gets when she has a mystery she wants to solve. I'm going to be really annoyed if it says something mundane like 'Grandma Hawthorn was here.'"

"I doubt your grandmother would have gone to the trouble of sealing the door unless it was important enough that she didn't want to risk anyone outside of your family getting in."

"Or anyone *inside* our family, at this rate." It wouldn't do any good to dwell on the matter without more clues, yet the question remained in my mind… what had Grandma wanted to hide?

And since when had she and my father shared a secret code?

2

After our walk, Xavier and I returned to the library to find Estelle had company in the form of Sylvester. The owl sat atop one of the shelves behind the front desk, looking down upon us like an imperial overlord surveying his domain. That wasn't entirely inaccurate, given his true nature.

"If it isn't the Reaper," Sylvester said. "Stolen any souls recently?"

"Don't be absurd," I said to him. "Xavier doesn't steal souls. He ferries them to the afterlife. What're you doing down here?"

"Can't I fly around my own library at will?"

I thought you were sulking. I squashed down the words and instead said, "I thought you'd be with Aunt Candace. Estelle, you told him what she's up to, right?"

Estelle grimaced. "I did, but he's not interested."

"I could not possibly care any less about that corridor," Sylvester announced. "Candace is welcome to it."

Uh-huh. "I assume you'd feel differently about any other part of the library."

I probably shouldn't push the issue, given the owl's notoriously fickle nature and temperament, but before he could reply, Xavier went completely still, his gaze fixed at a point in the distance as if he was looking at something far away.

"Xavier?"

His gaze sharpened. "I'm being called to collect a soul."

And he was gone, in a blur of darkness. A surprised silence lingered in his wake.

Sylvester interrupted with a hoot that sounded like a laugh. "Rather a dramatic way to get out of spending any more time in your company."

"Very funny." My spine prickled. *Who died?* The death could have been completely natural and expected, but in my experience, coincidences were rare when it came to the Reaper's fine-tuned sense for death. My instinct told me to follow him, but that rarely ended well either.

"Weird." Unease flickered across Estelle's expression. "I'm sure it's nothing."

"Was that Xavier?" Aunt Adelaide came walking into view, her gaze on the door. "Sorry I missed him."

"How're the taxes going?" I asked.

"Slowly." She ducked behind the desk, retrieved one of the library's record books, and tucked it under her arm. Like her daughter, my aunt Adelaide had long curly red hair and a curvy frame, and she wore the same black cloak embossed with our family's crest—two crossed pens above an owl sitting atop an open book. "Your aunt is *not* helping matters. Did you know she tried to claim the new coffee maker as a business expense?"

"She didn't, did she?" Estelle groaned. "At least you caught it before we got into trouble."

"Yes, and I suppose I can thank that corridor for distracting her from trying to 'help' me with the paperwork."

She tutted. "She always manages to complicate matters even more than they already are."

At the mention of the corridor, Sylvester made a rude noise and shuffled along the shelf he was perched on.

"How much longer do you think it'll take?" I asked my aunt, ignoring the owl.

"A couple of days, with luck. I should get back to it."

She retreated while Sylvester's head rotated to follow her movements. I suspected he knew exactly how freaky it looked when he did that.

"I hope Aunt Candace hasn't made things too difficult," I told Estelle. "A coffee maker? Really?"

"She always tries to write off ridiculous things as business expenses," Estelle replied. "Last time, it was shoes."

"Those are technically essential for the job," Sylvester put in. "Especially in the Walking on Hot Coals Section."

"That's not a thing. You just made that up."

A buzzing noise interrupted Sylvester's reply, and Estelle fished her phone out of her pocket. "Oh, it's someone from uni. Hang on."

As she backed away to take the call, the library's door opened, and a pair of young women entered, carrying a stack of books to return. I hastened to help them before Sylvester decided to freak them out by spinning his head around again, and by the time I was finished, Estelle had returned to the desk. She'd gone pale, her eyes wide. "He's dead."

"Who?" My heart gave a lurch, and the memory of Xavier's sudden departure sprang to mind. "Who's dead?"

"My PhD supervisor." She put her phone on the desk and dragged a hand through her hair. "Professor Booker. I was just talking to him less than an hour ago."

"He was the one whose soul Xavier was called to collect?" Ivory Beach was small enough that two deaths in the space of an hour would be a rare occurrence.

"Must have been." She rested her palms on either side of her phone, her head drooping over the desk. "I don't get it. They said he just collapsed and died, out of nowhere. A student found him."

"I'm sorry." I didn't quite know what to say, so I settled for putting an arm around her. "Maybe… maybe they haven't figured out what happened yet."

Her shoulders trembled, and she lifted her head, showing eyes brimming over with tears. "He wasn't that old, there was nothing wrong with him… and we just spoke. He was alive an hour ago."

"That's usually how it is," Sylvester said helpfully. "Why are humans so surprised when natural processes take their course?"

"Go away." I waved a hand at him. "Make yourself useful and help Aunt Candace with her mystery code or something."

Sylvester retreated with an indignant hoot, and I pulled Estelle into an awkward hug. She buried her face in my shoulder with a muffled sob.

A short while later, Estelle lifted her head and wiped her eyes on the back of her hand. "Thanks, Rory. I… I don't know how to handle this. How can he be dead?"

"Was he the professor you were going to ask about Aunt Candace's code?" A jolt of suspicion seized me, but I pushed it down.

"Yes." She took out her wand and conjured up a handkerchief. "Yes, and he… he said he'd look into it for me."

My suspicions multiplied, but I bit my tongue. If someone I'd been close to had died, I wouldn't have appreciated anyone making insinuations about their cause of death… but what if my suspicions were close to the mark? "Ah—if you want me to, I can ask Xavier."

"Ask him what?" She blew her nose. "He—he collected

Professor Booker's soul. You don't think he might have spoken to him, asked how he died?"

"He doesn't usually, but I can ask. He won't mind."

Xavier's boss might, but he didn't have to know. The Grim Reaper, unlike his apprentice, had zero grasp of human emotions. He wouldn't care if Estelle was concerned about her mentor's death; as far as he was concerned, humans were another species and only worth associating with when a Reaper had to escort one of their souls to the afterlife. Then again, he'd somehow agreed to let Xavier have a relationship with me, and I figured it was worth asking Xavier when we met up for a date we'd scheduled for that evening.

"It's fine." Estelle sniffed. "Really, it's probably nothing out of the ordinary. I just didn't want to believe it."

"I get it." I remembered how it'd felt when I'd first got the news about Dad. A phone call on a Friday evening in winter telling me of the car crash that had taken both his life and that of the drunk driver who'd ploughed into him on an icy road. "It's a shock when it comes out of nowhere."

My mother's death from cancer, I'd been able to prepare for—as much as a teenager could prepare for losing their mother, anyway—but my dad's had knocked the foundations out from underneath my life, and not until I'd moved to the library had I realised that I'd been living in the shadow of that loss without fully knowing it. This was likely the first time Estelle had lost someone close—aside from Grandma, but that had been years ago, when she was a baby.

Estelle took in a shuddering breath. "I guess it is. I'm sorry."

"Don't apologise," I protested. "Tell you what—I'll watch the desk. It's quiet enough that I can handle things alone."

"Are you sure?" She rubbed her eyes.

"Of course," I insisted. "I'll text Xavier, too, but we're meeting for dinner this evening anyway."

"Thanks, Rory." She hugged me again and then crossed the lobby to the living quarters while I sat back behind the desk and hoped I wasn't tempting a whole group of patrons to show up with unreasonable demands. Especially now I'd driven off Sylvester.

A few minutes later, Aunt Adelaide came walking into view. "Rory… what's wrong with Estelle?"

"Her PhD supervisor died," I explained. "Xavier was just called to collect his soul. She's pretty shaken up."

"Oh no." Her face fell. "I'll talk to her."

I watched her depart, hoping I wasn't making a mistake by asking Xavier for the details. He'd be able to confirm if anything strange was involved in Professor Booker's death, but if there was, it'd be cold comfort for Estelle.

Yet I couldn't forget that Estelle had called Professor Booker to discuss our grandmother's coding spell not an hour before his death.

The rest of the day raced by, between helping clients and watching the desk. I could theoretically have taken a few minutes to write more words in my journal, but my head wasn't in the right place for it. I kept thinking of Aunt Candace working on Grandma's code in the back room and the knowledge that a man had died shortly after Estelle had called him to discuss that very subject.

Coincidence or not? It wouldn't be the first time our family's secrets had got someone killed, and suspicions gnawed at me throughout the rest of the afternoon. Even getting through half a day of singlehandedly watching the library with nothing going wrong filled me with less pride than it might once have.

Aunt Candace finally made a reappearance as I was

closing the library for the evening. She strode out of the classroom, carrying the whiff of a burning smell and with her eyebrows singed clean off.

"I take it you didn't manage to crack the code?" I called after her as she vanished into the living quarters. "Ah—can I have my spell back?"

"Not yet," she said over her shoulder. "I'm almost there, I'm sure."

Right. I returned to tidying the desk while I waited for Xavier, and the Reaper arrived a few minutes later with his customary knock on the door.

"You don't have to do that, you know." I greeted him with a kiss. "Everything okay?"

"My boss is trying to guilt-trip me about going out in the evenings again," he replied. "I told him that I'm more than attentive enough when I'm doing my job, but you know what he's like."

I did. Unfortunately. "He did let you come out on a date, though."

"He might be a grump, but he keeps his promises." He slid his hand into mine, and we walked out into the cool evening air again.

While we crossed the square towards the seafront, I steeled myself to ask the question.

"Xavier, about that soul you were called to collect earlier," I began. "Ah, was it from the university?"

"Yes—how did you know?" he asked.

"Estelle," I answered. "She said the man who died was her supervisor who helped her with her PhD, so she's pretty upset."

"Oh." His mouth turned down at the corners. "I'm sorry for that. It looked like his death was painless, if it's any consolation."

"She said he dropped dead without any cause," I added. "Did you talk to him?"

"No, he crossed over too quickly," he replied. "Why? Did Estelle want me to speak to him?"

"Not exactly," I said, "but she called him an hour before his death to ask him about… about that code Aunt Candace found."

"Huh." A crease appeared in his brow. "I can't say anything seemed suspicious at the time, but I did think it odd that he died in a lab."

"One of the campus labs?" I pictured a room full of billowing smoke and a large cauldron, with a sign on the door reading Secret Lab. "What was he doing in there?"

"I don't know, but I found him lying on the floor," Xavier said. "There was a broken glass bottle next to him. The contents had spilled, but I don't know enough about potions to have any idea what it was."

"Anyone else in the room?"

"No," he answered. "Not that I know of. I got out of there pretty fast. I'm not supposed to interact with anyone else when I collect the dead."

"Guess not." Wouldn't someone have called the police if they'd suspected foul play? "I wonder—are they going to do an autopsy or anything?"

"I can find out." As we walked out onto the seafront, he gazed at the police station that lay across from the beach. "Maybe not now, though. We don't need to ruin Edwin's evening, and the word of the Reaper isn't evidence by itself. Not when the professor's death looked like an accident."

"Even though he dropped dead in a lab?" Granted, the head of the police wouldn't be thrilled at us for dropping another bombshell on him. "If he was poisoned or something… I guess that could still be accidental, but the timing is weird."

"An awful lot of toxic-looking substances were in that room," he remarked. "I guess that's what you expect of a professor who deals with magical potions."

"I don't remember Estelle's PhD having anything to do with alchemy or potions," I said. "And she mentioned that he was an expert on codes, not poultices."

What would he have been doing in the lab, then? Maybe it was worth looking into, but I'd have to see what Estelle thought.

"I didn't know him," he said. "He didn't say anything before I collected his soul either. He just looked confused. If I'd asked him a question or two, it might have helped, but most ghosts in that kind of state are too out of it to even know they're dead."

"You couldn't have known." I squeezed his hand. "I'm sure Estelle will talk to the university staff, and if she thinks there's something off with his death, it'll be easier for her to get in touch with the police than for you to risk annoying your boss."

"It's not much of a risk," he said. "Being able to walk through walls comes in handy. But you're right. If Estelle wants closure, she's better off talking to the university staff herself than relying on a Reaper."

"I wonder if he knew Professor Colt?" I recalled the professor whom my dad had entrusted with a dangerous book he'd wanted to keep from the Founders. That book was now safely stored in our library, but Professor Colt had since left town out of a concern for his own safety.

Xavier grimaced. "I don't know that we can make any assumptions. The professor isn't in town anymore, I thought."

"He isn't, but the other staff knew him." Maybe I was being paranoid… but I had to wonder. "Never mind. It's not my business, and I should be more concerned about Aunt

Candace and what she might unleash next. She burned her eyebrows off earlier."

We entered the restaurant and took our seats at a table, debating over what Aunt Candace might need to do to translate an unreadable code.

"It's overly complicated even by my grandmother's standards," I added. "Unfortunately, my aunt's taken it as a personal challenge, but I guess it'll keep her out of trouble. So far, her eyebrows have been the only casualty."

"She'll live, I'm sure." Xavier picked up the menu and selected his order with a tap of his fingers. "Has she actually published anything since she found that corridor?"

"You know, I'm not sure she has." I ordered my own food, all too happy to put the subject of the professor's death out of my mind and discuss more pleasant topics for the rest of our date.

At the end of the evening, the two of us walked back to the library in good spirits. In the lobby, I found Laney, my best friend, waiting beside the desk with the typical elegant stillness of a vampire.

"Oh." I came to a halt, certain that her vampire hearing had picked up on the way my heart had jumped into my throat. "Hey, Laney."

"Hey, Rory," she said. "Hey, Xavier. What's up with your cousin? She seemed really upset."

"Estelle?" Laney could easily have read her thoughts if she wanted to, but I guessed she'd wanted to be polite. "Her supervisor died. The guy who helped with her PhD."

"Oh, that's a shame," she said. "I didn't want to read her thoughts, but I wondered why she was making so many phone calls."

"To campus?" She'd likely find out that his body had been found in the lab, and it was up to her whether she wanted to open an investigation or contact the police.

"Yeah, I thought so. She knows pretty much all the staff up there."

"Uh-huh." She glided around the desk, her movements uncharacteristically hesitant.

"Do you have a lesson this evening?" I asked her. "Or…?"

"I've been given a mission," Laney said, not meeting my eyes. "Outside town. I figured you'd want to know before I leave."

"Evangeline's sending you after the Founders." Fear trickled down my spine. "Isn't she?"

"Only to scout their possible locations," she replied. "If I do find them, I won't be showing my face."

Still. As a vampire, Laney was more resilient than most people, but so were the Founders, and they had years of experience on her. Decades or centuries, even. Evangeline knew that perfectly well, but she'd taken Laney under her wing and gave her little choice but to rely upon her generosity for her undead existence.

"I'll be fine," Laney said. "I wanted to tell you, but don't wait up for me. I'll be back by morning. You can knock on my door and check on me."

"All right." My voice wavered, fear a clenched fist in my chest. "Stay safe, okay?"

She gave me a wave and vanished through the door, and Xavier took my hand. "I'm sure she'll be fine."

"I *hope* so." I released a shaky breath. "I know I should get used to this. I mean, she's pretty far into her vampire training, and it's unreasonable to expect her to stay in the library, reading books instead of wandering around at night."

"There is that," said Xavier. "I prefer staying in and reading books, personally."

"You're just saying that because you know *I* like that." I gave him a wavering smile. "You'd rather be out stalking souls in the dark."

"That's my nature as a Reaper, but I'm not opposed to staying in and doing human things instead." He kissed me, and I eased into his embrace. The feeling didn't quite erase my worry for Laney, but I'd have to trust that she could take care of herself out there. She'd always been more self-sufficient than me, and while vampires weren't invulnerable, they were hard to leave a mark on.

Of course, I would be less tuned in to their few weaknesses if I hadn't spent the past few months researching how to kill one. Luckily, most vampires would never employ those tactics against their own kind. Laney had been an exception, and when she'd staked two Founders to death, Evangeline had swooped in and promised to protect her from their wrath.

Now, it seemed, she was sending her into the lion's den regardless.

Please be careful out there, Laney.

3

The following morning, I knocked on Laney's door as planned to ask how Evangeline's mission had gone. Laney replied blearily that she'd had no luck finding any traces of the Founders, and it was all I could do to conceal my relief. I'd have to get more details from her when she woke up that evening, because she fell asleep again an instant later. Sometimes, I envied the vampires their ability to effortlessly fall into a coma-like sleep at the drop of a hat, because my own night had been restless and disturbed.

Yawning, I went downstairs to get breakfast, where I found Estelle pacing the living room, clutching her phone in one hand. She gave me a wan smile and joined me in the kitchen. Aunt Adelaide had left a pot of coffee and a note saying she'd gone to deal with the taxes early so she'd be mostly finished before the library started getting a lot of visitors.

"Wise idea," I said, sliding bread into the toaster. "Everything okay, Estelle?"

Estelle had sat down at the table with her gaze on her phone screen, but at my question, she lifted her head. "I've been asked to come up to campus to sort out some of Professor Booker's things. He's supposed to be supervising a bunch of other students with their theses, and I'm one of the few people who knows where everything in his office is. Is that okay with you?"

"Me? Of course, it's okay. I don't mind watching the desk while you're out, and your mum will be done with taxes soon, won't she? Assuming Aunt Candace hasn't left her any more unwelcome surprises in the paperwork."

"Yeah…" She sighed. "It's complete chaos over on campus. It's terrible timing, a professor dying right at the start of the academic year. I was thinking of volunteering to teach some of his seminars myself, but I know it's not fair on the rest of you."

The toast popped up. I removed it from the toaster and placed two more slices inside. "If Aunt Candace and Cass stepped up once in a while, it wouldn't be an issue. You should do whatever you feel like."

"I don't see either of them stepping up to run the poetry night, do you?" She began pouring out coffee for both of us. "I'm still mildly scarred from the few times Aunt Candace has stepped in."

"The poetry night is in the evening, right?" I grabbed the jam jar and set our plates on the table. "You won't be asked to run seminars after hours, I wouldn't have thought."

"No." She dragged a hand through her hair. "I barely slept last night. I'm losing my grip."

"You had a rough day yesterday." I finished pouring the coffee for her and joined her at the table. "If you want me to come with you to campus for moral support, I can do that. I'll bribe Aunt Candace to watch the desk. It's not like she's getting any writing done."

She hadn't returned the translator spell yet, either, but I

hadn't expected her to give it up until she'd exhausted all possible options for solving Grandma's riddle.

Estelle gave me a faint smile. "Might have to take you up on that one. I like the university, but some of the staff can be a bit much to deal with. Not to mention the students."

"I bet." My thoughts drifted back to what Xavier had said yesterday, that Professor Booker's body was found in a lab with a shattered bottle of some unknown liquid spilled next to him. I hadn't mentioned the details to Estelle yet, but none of those elements necessarily meant our suspicions were valid. "What was Professor Booker like? I know he helped you a lot."

"He was a bit more grounded than some of the other teachers." Her smile faded. "Always willing to go out of his way for his students. That's more than I can say for the professors who liked to lock themselves up in their offices to conduct magical experiments or just laze around instead of working."

"What department was he in again? Not—?" I broke off, unsure if I'd make the situation worse by mentioning what Xavier had said. On the other hand, if I were in her place, I'd want to know the truth.

"Magical theory, but he helped pretty much anyone if their subject interested him enough," she replied. "They didn't have to be from his own department."

"So… it'd be unusual for him to be in the alchemy labs?" I decided to plunge ahead. "That was where he was when he died. Xavier told me."

Her mouth dropped open. "What? Nobody told me that. What on earth was he doing in there?"

"I wish I knew." I hesitated. "I don't want to pry where I'm not supposed to, but I figured you might want Xavier to tell you what he saw at the scene…"

"Rory, don't be absurd," she said. "It's not prying, and you're right, that *is* strange. What else did Xavier tell you?"

"He said there was a spilled potion on the floor when he walked in, but he didn't know what it was," I said. "I'm guessing they'll have cleaned it up by now… I also didn't ask him *which* lab, but I can message him again."

"No, it's fine. I'll ask on campus," she said. "I think I'd prefer to avoid getting on the Grim Reaper's bad side."

"He's used to me annoying him," I reminded her. "If you're sure, we can ask some questions on campus. Has anyone else mentioned having any… any suspicions about his death?"

"No." Her head dipped. "No, but why would they? They didn't hear me call him to ask about our grandmother's ridiculous riddle. They don't know we've ticked off the Founders, either, but—oh, Rory, what if my asking questions got him killed?"

"You didn't get him killed," I insisted. "He was found in a lab full of dangerous magical substances. His death might have nothing to do with the library."

"I guess all I can do is ask." Estelle dropped her gaze, her shoulders hunching. "I don't like this, but I hate not knowing the truth even more. I feel like I owe it to Professor Booker to find out."

So do I. After all, Grandma's riddle might have been what had led to his demise.

After we'd finished breakfast, we bribed Aunt Candace into watching the desk by means of loaning her my dad's journal—which I might regret later, but there was no chance I'd leave Estelle to go to the campus alone.

"I'll probably regret letting Aunt Candace borrow my dad's journal all morning," I told Estelle as we crossed the square. "But I figured she'd want to compare his code with the one Grandma wrote on the door, and we should get back before the library opens for the day."

"I hope so," Estelle said distractedly. "We should have asked Sylvester. He's easier to bribe—or he used to be."

"Before the fourth-floor corridor showed up." Now the owl was flightier than ever. Pun intended.

"Let's hope that translation spell will keep her distracted from poking around campus herself." Estelle turned into the high street branching off the square. "I didn't tell her that Professor Booker might have been able to figure out how to break the spell Grandma put on the door. If I had, she might have followed us in the hopes of finding some of his notes."

"What, he might have seen it before?" Unease skittered down my spine, but I was sure Professor Booker had never seen the door—or my dad's journal. "I didn't know anyone on campus was an expert on translations, but I didn't really ask. I was kind of trying to forget the whole business with Professor Colt and that book, to be honest."

"Yeah." Estelle ducked her head as wind gusted behind us up the high street. "I don't think Professor Booker ever set eyes on that code, and Professor Colt left town."

"To avoid... them." The Founders. Everything seemed to come back to the vampires, and I wished the professor *had* stayed in town so I could ask him a few questions. I didn't know anyone else who worked on campus who might know if the Founders had made any recent moves.

Estelle's expression grew grimmer as we walked past the church at the top of the high street where the vampires made their home. I averted my eyes out of habit—though Evangeline would be sleeping at this time of day—and followed Estelle towards the high fences surrounding the town's only university campus.

The campus reminded me of a Lego model assembled by a child who'd got bored halfway through construction; the buildings' sizes varied from towering blocks to more shed-sized constructions, and their appearances ranged from elaborate halls to dilapidated buildings with missing roof tiles and cracked windows.

We entered through the gates and headed to one of the nicer-looking brick buildings, three storeys high with a gilt-framed sign declaring it the Magical Theory Department. Inside, doors lined a blue-carpeted corridor, and Estelle paced ahead until she halted at one of the doors.

"I don't know if anyone else has been inside yet." She reached for the handle then startled when the door next to it swung open.

A well-dressed woman in a smart suit and skirt emerged to study the pair of us. From the bags under her bloodshot eyes, I hazarded a guess that she'd been one of Professor Booker's colleagues.

"Oh—Professor Quinn." Estelle stepped back from Professor Booker's office door. "Sorry, I thought I'd drop by to help. Someone messaged me and said there were a bunch of students who needed reassigning to another supervisor..."

"Of course there are," Professor Quinn said thickly. "It's a mess, frankly... such an awful thing."

"I know." Estelle swallowed. "Ah—this is my cousin, Rory. She works at the library, too, and she's interested in maybe studying here at some point."

She wasn't lying, but my knowledge was far behind that of most witches of my age thanks to my recent introduction to the magical world, and it'd be years before I'd reach the higher education level.

"Nice to meet you, Rory," Professor Quinn said. "Sorry. I'd have recommended you talk to Professor Booker if you have an interest in studying here, but..."

"Me too." Estelle's voice caught, and she cleared her throat a couple of times. "This might seem an odd question, but—where was the professor when they found him? Someone told me he was in the alchemy labs, which seems unlikely. Was he?"

"He was." Averting Estelle's gaze, Professor Quinn reached into her pocket and pulled out a handkerchief. "A—a student found him, and they flagged down the nearest member of staff."

"Why was he in the lab to begin with?" Estelle glanced at me, her expression conflicted. "Did he talk to you before he left?"

"No—I hadn't a clue." She blew her nose. "I didn't watch him all the time, did I?"

Her tone had more bite in it than I thought the situation warranted, but she was obviously rather upset. Professor Booker had been her colleague, after all, and his office had been right next to hers, so they must have seen each other frequently.

"Of course not," Estelle said. "I just wondered… I mean, I called him not an hour before he died, and he was in his office at the time."

"You called him?" She regarded both of us with watery eyes. "Why?"

"I had a question that I thought he might be able to answer, but he couldn't," Estelle said carefully. "Library stuff, you know."

"Right." The professor gave me an odd look. "Is there a reason you both came here today?"

"Oh, I brought Rory to have a look around while I'm sorting out Professor Booker's schedule," Estelle said. "I was going to offer to run some seminars… unless someone else has already volunteered?"

"Oh, no," she said. "Nobody has. He was so particular that no one has dared touch anything in his office yet. I wouldn't want anything to go missing."

"They haven't?" A slight hint of tension underlay Estelle's words. "Did—sorry, did the police come here yesterday, or just the emergency services?"

"Not the police, no." Professor Quinn's frown deepened. "Why would they?"

"I just wondered if anyone else had been in his office, but it'll be easier if they haven't." Estelle moved towards the door, and so did Professor Quinn. If she intended to follow, I wouldn't be able to get away with talking to Estelle about our shared suspicions—not if we didn't want anyone else to know yet.

Estelle gave me a tight smile. "You can look around while I'm in here, Rory. You know some of the way round, right? Most places are signposted."

Did she mean the labs? I *had* been in that building before, a while ago, but I couldn't guarantee I'd be able to find my way on my own.

"It's all right. Nobody will mind," she added. "Just say you're with me."

I had my doubts; I had no good reason to be there, and I didn't have a Reaper's ability to walk through walls either. But the other professor had the air of someone who'd wanted to find out what was inside Professor Booker's office but had been too polite to ask, and she showed no signs of budging. *What a pain.*

"All right. I'll be back soon," I said, resigned.

"I'll come and find you." Estelle waved at me, and I left the building to track down the labs.

The squarish building turned out to be easy to find once I'd got my bearings. I pushed open the door carefully, inhaling the scent of burning herbs that seemed to permeate every inch of the place. My last visit had been a brief one, when I'd been searching for someone responsible for brewing an illegal potion, but I knew my way to the door marked by the self-explanatory sign reading Secret Lab. Someone had taken down the protective wards that usually covered the outside, but otherwise, the slightly singed wooden door hadn't changed. I took in a deep breath and pushed on the handle.

No magical explosions greeted me. Neither did any person, student or staff. A cauldron dominated the back of the room—probably the same one Nova Lyle had used to brew dodgy love potions—but someone must have emptied its contents. Various bottles and jars stood on the shelves, but I wouldn't know one potion from another if they belonged to advanced experimental alchemy far beyond my own magical education.

My gaze went straight to the grimy floor, but if Professor Booker had indeed died in here, there were no signs of the broken bottle and its spilled contents that Xavier had seen. Layers of burn marks and stains overlapped on the floor, the results of years of spilled potions and exploding cauldrons. It'd be impossible to identify one stain amid a thousand.

Creaking footsteps sounded outside. I stiffened and turned around as the door opened and an older woman with grey hair entered. She looked down at me through her wide spectacles. "What are you doing in here?"

"Sorry, I was—looking for a potion, but it's not in here." I should have rehearsed an excuse before I came in, but the empty room had taken me off guard.

"Are you a student here?" asked the woman. "You don't look familiar."

"I'm—my cousin was a student here until recently," I said, truthfully enough. "She sent me to run an errand. Estelle Hawthorn."

"Oh, her." She pursed her lips. "One of Charles Booker's proteges."

Her tone was decidedly not respectful towards someone

who'd died the previous day. "Yes… he died, didn't he?"

"Such a shame." She didn't sound sorry either. "You're not supposed to be in here. Tell your cousin that she can't send her relatives wandering into the labs. You might pick up something you're not supposed to."

Did she mean to sound as threatening as she did? Quite possibly, yes. While part of me quailed at the idea of ticking off a teacher, even though my school days were long behind me, I pushed the instinct aside. "I haven't touched anything. Why, did Professor Booker die in here?"

She looked askance at me. "Yes, he did. Foolish man."

"What does that mean?" I shuffled through the questions in my mind and found the most pertinent one. "I thought his death was an accident…"

"Did your cousin tell you that?" Her disdain deepened. "Tell her to hold her tongue around her family members. It'll get her into trouble someday."

What did *that* mean? "She liked Professor Booker. She's very upset that he died."

The woman made an unimpressed sound. "Yes, I expect she is. Go on, get out of here. I'm not paid to turf out trespassers."

"Do you get a lot of those?" A rare spark of daring rose inside me, despite myself.

"Of course not." Another unimpressed snort. "The campus is as secure as anywhere. The most trouble is more likely to come from inside. Go on, shoo."

I gave up on arguing and resigned myself to waiting for Estelle out in the cold. Clearly, I wouldn't be allowed to do any more snooping, so I left the unfriendly woman to her lab and walked outside.

Was she the one who found Professor Booker's body? No, Professor Quinn had said it'd been a student. Speaking of whom, I wondered if she'd left Estelle alone yet.

I dawdled on the way back to the building then sped up when I saw my cousin approaching from that direction.

"Hey, Rory." Estelle hurried up to me. "You found the right place?"

"Until I got thrown out for trespassing." I lowered my voice. "You managed to ditch Professor Quinn, then?"

"Yes… she means well, but I don't want to drag her into this if I can help it," she said. "Who threw you out?"

"An older professor who works in there," I replied. "At least, I think she does. She didn't say."

"Not Dr Hayes." Estelle rolled her eyes. "Sorry. I should have come with you."

"She didn't seem to like Professor Booker much. Or…"

"Me?" Estelle snorted. "She doesn't like anyone, pretty much. I forgot she'd be hanging around the place."

"Do you think she might have been the one Professor Booker's death was reported to?" I asked. "I know Professor Quinn said it was a student who found him…"

Estelle winced. "Yes, and I found out which student too. Jesse Rogan, our resident troublemaker."

Did Estelle know everyone on campus? "A troublemaker, you say?"

"Yes, he's notorious," she said. "He got dinged for plagiarism as an undergraduate while I was doing my PhD. Hard to forget that kind of thing."

"Who caught him out?" I suspected I knew the answer, somehow.

"Professor Booker did," she said. "I wonder why he was on campus? I thought he got kicked out."

"He did?" Suspicion brewed inside me. "He came back and just happened to find a dead body?"

"He used to spend all his time in the labs when he was here." Estelle paused. "Yeah, I think we should find him."

4

We'd barely been on campus for half an hour, and we already had two possible suspects? Not that either of us knew how to find a troublemaking wizard who'd been expelled months ago. Estelle flagged down a passing witch with green hair and asked, "Excuse me—do you know if Jesse Rogan is around?"

"Jesse Rogan?" the witch echoed. "Wasn't he expelled?"

"Yes, but I heard he was on campus," said Estelle. "I wanted to make sure he isn't causing trouble."

"If he's on campus, I can guarantee that's exactly what he's doing, but I haven't seen him," the witch said. "Sorry."

"I see what you mean about him being notorious," I muttered to Estelle as the witch ambled away. "Does everyone here know who he is?"

"Pretty much," she replied. "We always get at least one case of plagiarism in each batch of students, but that guy somehow managed to copy someone else's essay without even setting foot in the same room as them."

"That seems… concerning."

"I still don't know how he did it." She shook her head.

"The university doesn't kick people out without good reason, and he'd already had two warnings. He doesn't live in campus accommodation any longer, so I'm not sure where to find him if he isn't here."

"The university has his contact details, right?"

"I'll check later. We should head back to the library. I don't think we're going to find anything else… here…" She trailed off.

"Estelle?" I followed her gaze to the building opposite us, which contained the campus's designated learning area, where the students often hung out between lectures. Bean-bags and tables occupied a large, airy space. Amid them, a young man stood on one of the tables. He held up a large briefcase, gesticulating wildly with his free hand as he addressed an unseen audience.

"Estelle?" I repeated. "You look like you've seen a ghost."

"That's him." She snapped out of her trance and marched towards the door. "Jesse Rogan. He's been right in front of our eyes the whole time."

That's Jesse Rogan? "So much for him being hard to get hold of."

The automatic doors slid open, and Estelle strode in, making a beeline for the table upon which Jesse Rogan stood.

"Have you ever felt that the system was stacked against you?" he asked in a booming voice, the result of some kind of amplification spell, but few people were paying him any attention. "Have you ever felt victimised by unfair grading policies? If so, you might benefit from my Spell Assistant. It'll bring your work to the next level by helping you write essays that fulfil the requirements while freeing up your mind for leisure activities…"

"Jesse," Estelle called over to him. "Are you supposed to be in here?"

"What?" Irritation cut across Jesse's face. "I'm busy. Can't you see that?"

"You've also not a student here," Estelle said pointedly. "Get down here before someone calls security."

He slammed the briefcase closed and hopped off the table. "Fine."

Several of the students booed or flashed rude gestures at him when he departed. Not popular with his peers, then.

"Wait." Estelle hastened to catch up to him at the doors. "I have a couple of questions I want to ask you."

"Thought you wanted me gone." He stalked out of the building, a scowl on his face. "You're not the boss here, you know."

"You found Professor Booker." Hesitation underlay her voice. "In the lab. Didn't you?"

"Yes, and?" He swivelled to her, taking on a combative stance. "Your point?"

"Why were you in the lab to begin with?" Estelle asked. "You aren't studying here any longer."

Jesse shrugged. "Just having a look around."

"Uh-huh." Estelle's usually friendly manner was completely absent, though I didn't blame her; I didn't much like the guy, either, and I'd only just met him. "If I gave you the benefit of the doubt, I'm assuming it's to do with what you have in that briefcase. What is that 'Spell Assistant' thing, exactly?"

Jesse's jaw locked. "It's mine. It doesn't belong to the university."

"I never said it did," Estelle said, "but if you were using supplies from the alchemy lab, those don't belong to you."

"How dare you call me a thief?" He drew himself upright. "You're discriminating, you are."

"You were literally kicked out of the university for plagiarism," Estelle retaliated. "For copying another student's paper without being in the same room. Did you use that Spell Assistant to do so, by any chance?"

"I couldn't have seen those papers, and you know it," Jesse retaliated. "Maybe we just had the same idea. You and that Professor Booker were conspiring against me. I could report you for that."

To whom? I bit down on the words; I didn't need to draw Jesse's ire when he was picking a fight with Estelle.

"I didn't want to kick anyone out, and I don't have the authority to make that call," Estelle said. "Professor Booker did, but you brought it on yourself by breaking the rules. He gave you a chance, and you blew it."

"It was a setup." His face flushed bright red. "Now you're trying to set me up again by accusing me of stealing."

"I'm not accusing you of stealing," Estelle said evenly, "but Professor Booker is dead, and since you were the one who found his body, you're the only person who can answer my questions. Was he the only person in the room when you found him?"

"Yes." Suspicion flickered in his eyes. "You're trying to say I killed him, aren't you?"

"No."

Jesse spun on his heel, the briefcase swinging in his hands, and Estelle held her ground. "No," she said, "but you can't deny it looks suspicious that you showed up in a lab you weren't supposed to be in, at the same time as someone died."

Oh boy. She was right, though. Might Jesse have retaliated against Professor Booker for kicking him out? Jesse certainly fit the criteria, but if he *was* the killer, why come back to campus and cause a ruckus in public?

"How dare you." Jesse moved close enough that he and Estelle stood nose to nose. "You'll pay for slandering me."

"Those were your words, not mine." Estelle's hand

reached towards her sleeve, where she kept her wand. "Back off, Jesse."

I pushed past my better instincts and spoke up. "If you're innocent, you won't mind answering questions. Such as what potion was spilled on the floor next to Professor Booker's body. You saw it, didn't you?"

He swivelled to me. "Who said anything about spilled potions?"

"The Reaper." I hadn't wanted to play that card, but I figured it was one of the few things that might get him to stop threatening my cousin.

As I'd hoped, Jesse's bravado faded at my words. "What Reaper?"

"The Reaper who collected Professor Booker's soul," I continued. "He was quite clear about what he saw. If you know anything about that potion, we'd all appreciate it if you told us the truth."

His mouth opened and closed like a goldfish's. "I… I don't know what it was."

"Are you sure about that?" Estelle shot me a grateful look then returned her attention to Jesse. "You remember it now, do you?"

"I don't know what it was, all right?" he said defensively. "I'm not an alchemy expert. It was probably harmless."

"You don't think it—or anything else in the lab—caused the professor's death?" Estelle queried.

"No. He wouldn't have drunk poison on purpose, would he?"

"Poison or not, what happened to the potion afterwards?" asked Estelle.

"I guess someone cleaned it up." He folded his arms across his chest, the briefcase dangling from one fist. "I dunno. I got the hell out of there when the paramedics showed up."

"Who else was there?" I asked, unable to believe the paramedics had simply let him leave without asking any questions. "Aside from Dr Hayes?"

"Her." His scowl deepened. "She was the one who told me to leave."

"There wasn't anyone else in the lab?" Estelle pressed.

"No, there wasn't." He unfolded his arms. "Not many people use those labs. That's all I know. Will you leave me alone now?"

Is that all you know? He'd shared enough to make me figure that he was telling the truth about the discovery of the body, at least... just not necessarily about everything that had led up to that moment.

"Yes, assuming you don't come back to campus again and implicate yourself," Estelle said. "You're lucky nobody called security to remove you."

"I'm allowed to walk in here," he said. "It's a free country."

"You're not allowed to sell things to the students," said Estelle. "What is that Spell Assistant, anyway? Where'd you get it?"

"None of your business." He spun around and walked towards the gates. I considered calling him back, but I was out of questions to ask for now, and I didn't want him to decide it was worth picking a fight with the Reaper.

"What're the odds that he's not being truthful?" I asked Estelle out of the corner of my mouth. "For that matter, why'd Dr Hayes order him to leave the lab without reporting his presence on campus to anyone?"

"That's a very good question." Her gaze went back in the direction of the labs. "I don't know that she'll be any more willing to talk to me than Jesse was, though."

"She might know about the potion that was spilled on the floor," I suggested. "And who cleaned it up."

"She might, but it'd have been the paramedics who removed Professor Booker's body from the scene," she replied. "They wouldn't have wanted to touch a potentially dangerous potion while they were getting him out of there, and the autopsy might reveal the cause of death without anyone needing to see the potion itself."

"If his death turns out to have been caused by some kind of substance in the lab, that wouldn't mean it wasn't an accident, would it?" I queried. "I mean, would it be enough for the police to open an investigation?"

"I'll see what Edwin thinks." She cast her gaze over the buildings, her curly red hair blowing sideways in the breeze. "I might call the hospital first. Ask about the autopsy and whether they plan to do any more tests..."

"It's worth a try," I said. "Want to head back to the library now?"

"Definitely. There's only so long we can leave Aunt Candace at the desk before she turns someone into a walrus again."

"Again?" I echoed. "She's done that before?"

"Once, when she wanted to double-check if her description in a book was accurate."

"I shouldn't have asked."

While my instincts told me we hadn't unearthed the full picture of the circumstances of Professor Booker's death yet, we didn't have proof his death had been anything but bad luck. Until we did, the police were unlikely to see the situation as worth investigating, and my family had a contentious relationship with the local police department at the best of times.

As for Jesse, even if he was innocent of murder, I had to wonder what he'd hoped to achieve by coming back to campus and trying to sell his plagiarism spell to the other students. A spell that had conjured up an exact copy of another student's essay without the owner ever setting eyes on it struck me as the kind of thing that belonged in the library. Like a more advanced version of Aunt Candace's translator spell. *Hmm.*

Estelle and I slowed down when we saw Jesse making his dawdling way to the exit too. From his exaggeratedly small steps, he seemed to be trying to set some kind of record for how slowly someone could walk through a gate. Upon seeing us behind him, he glared over his shoulder. "What?"

"We're leaving too," Estelle said. "Aren't you going outside? You don't want to get caught loitering by security."

He glowered but reluctantly picked up the pace. When we reached the other side of the gates, Estelle and I veered towards the high street, but he lingered behind, carrying the distinct air of someone intending to sneak back in through the gates the instant we were out of sight.

Estelle sighed, pulled out her phone, and tapped a few buttons. "Jesse, you can't go back in there. Or else I *will* call security."

He called her a rude name but resignedly sloped off down the street.

"Hope he got the message," I whispered. "You do have someone you can contact on campus if he comes back, right?"

"I do, but I don't want them wasting their time with Jesse if there's a killer on the loose," she said in a low voice.

"Assuming he isn't the killer himself?" There was no good reason that he'd been in the lab when he'd found the professor's body. "Can't you… I don't know, call his parents or something?"

"He's over eighteen, so they might not be able to help," she commented. "I'll warn everyone I know on campus and see what they can do."

She sent off message after message while we walked back to the library. It was almost nine, but nobody was at the front desk when we walked in.

Estelle put her phone away. "Where'd Aunt Candace run off to?"

"The third floor," I guessed. "Or her research cave with the translation spell. One or the other."

She'd also taken my dad's journal, which I was already regretting loaning her.

"I'll tell my mother." Estelle made for the back rooms, and I looked up at the balconies overlooking the ground floor, craning my neck to see if Aunt Candace was upstairs. Three storeys of bookcases loomed overhead, while the fourth floor wasn't visible at all.

I called for my familiar. "Jet?"

After a moment, the little crow came swooping down from above. "Here, partner! Your aunt is upstairs."

"Of course, she is." I followed him up one of the winding staircases in the lobby. "Didn't you tell her to open the library?"

"She said she had an emergency, partner!" the little crow squeaked.

"An emergency?" I shook my head, ascending the next staircase. "If this is a real emergency, I'm a unicorn."

When we reached the third floor, Jet flew ahead of me above the towering shelves. I proceeded to the open door near which Aunt Candace sat, perched on a beanbag with the translation spell balanced on her knees. A foul stench emanated from somewhere nearby.

"What's this?" I wrinkled my nose. "What did the code do, turn into manticore dung when you tried to translate it?"

"Not quite." Cass stepped into view from near the door to the Magical Creatures Division. Her hair was tied into a messy bun, her glasses were off, and the smell of dung rolled off her. "It turned her purple. I had to come out to turn her back."

"Some emergency that was." I covered my nose with my

hand. "Aunt Candace, you're supposed to be watching the desk."

"Now, that's not very nice of you," she said. "I'm finally making progress, and you come up here and lecture me?"

"Where's my dad's journal?" I extended a hand. "I agreed to loan it to you in exchange for watching the door, and evidently, you didn't want it badly enough. Also, you'd better not have turned *that* purple too."

"Ooh." When I gave her a pointed stare, she reached into her pocket and pulled out the journal—which, luckily, apparently hadn't turned purple. "I don't know what the problem is. There are more than enough people to watch the library now that you and Estelle are back from your errand."

"Errand?" I took the journal back. "Weren't you listening to us earlier? We're pretty sure Estelle's professor was murdered."

I'd figured that'd get her attention; nothing captured my aunt's focus quite like a good story. "Nobody mentioned murder."

"What have you got yourself into this time?" Cass wanted to know. "Need me to set the manticore on someone? Because he's out of his cage already, so now's an excellent time."

"Well..." Jesse Rogan, for one, would deserve it, but I wouldn't subject the rest of campus to the wrath of a rampaging manticore. They'd had enough trauma this week already. "What do you mean he's out of his cage?"

"It's cleaning day, and he's very well-behaved," she replied. "Don't change the subject. Estelle's professor was murdered, right?"

"That's what we want to find out, but it'll be tricky for us to find time to talk to the police with you two slacking off up here when you're supposed to be working."

"I thought you didn't want me to leave the manticore

unattended," Cass said. "I can bring him downstairs if you'd rather."

"She's right, you know," said Aunt Candace.

"You don't have an excuse." I beckoned to my aunt. "Come on."

"You're developing quite the temperament." Aunt Candace resignedly picked up the translator spell and followed me to the stairs. "I blame that vampire friend of yours."

"Laney and I have been friends for most of our lives, Aunt Candace," I informed her. "You're likelier to be the bad influence on me."

"Or me." Cass returned to the door to the Magical Creatures Division. "Let me know if you need me to set the manticore on someone. He's getting a bit restless."

"Please don't send him out for exercise in the library," I called after her. To Aunt Candace, I remarked, "She's in an odd mood today."

"She's spending too much time next to that corridor." Aunt Candace sauntered around the corner. "It eats at the brain."

"Speak for yourself." I followed her, tucking my dad's journal back into my pocket. "Why'd you need to come up here in the first place? Couldn't you have asked Aunt Adelaide to undo the spell that turned you purple?"

"Yes, but I wanted to show the code to the guardian."

I nearly tripped over my own feet. "I'm starting to think you actually do want to lose your memory again."

"That's no danger," she said over her shoulder. "The guardian and I are very good friends now."

"Friends." Could one make friends with the ghostly embodiment of our grandmother's manifestation curse, created for the sole purpose of preventing anyone from breaking into the fourth-floor corridor? Well, if anyone was bound to try, it was Aunt Candace. "Did she have anything to say about the code?"

"Nothing whatsoever." She strode ahead of me, her hair bouncing on her shoulders. "That is an answer itself, isn't it?"

"No," I said. "No, it really isn't."

Unless Grandma hadn't even told her magical guardian what was behind the door, which was highly unlikely. No, this was part of the riddle, and it wasn't something I was inclined to get involved with. A murder to solve was quite enough on its own.

5

Estelle and I didn't have much time for sleuthing, though, between running the library and stopping Aunt Candace from wandering back upstairs again. Once I'd filled Aunt Candace in on the details of Professor Booker's death and our visit to campus, some of her interest had worn off. After all, we didn't have proof his death *was* a murder. Nor did we have a substantial idea of whether there was a connection with Estelle's call earlier that same day.

"Do you think someone tapped your phone?" Aunt Candace queried. "Or an axe-murderer was listening in?"

"He was killed by poison, not an axe-murderer—we think." Estelle snatched her phone out of Aunt Candace's reach. "Nobody is listening through my phone. Where'd you get that idea?"

"You have no imagination." Aunt Candace tutted. "Pity. Did this professor have anything useful to tell you before his unfortunate demise?"

"Aunt Candace, you have all the sympathy of a rampaging manticore," I said with a worried glance at Estelle. "And no, we already told you that he didn't know how to solve Grandma's latest riddle."

"He mentioned that the last similar case he heard of involved a book that melted the eyeballs of anyone who read it," Estelle told Aunt Candace. "I'm glad Grandma picked a slightly less hazardous security measure… Oh, what is it now?"

Estelle's phone buzzed, and she vanished amid the shelves, leaving me alone with Aunt Candace. This was typical; people had been calling from the university all morning, so she had to keep dashing off and leaving me to manage the desk and keep Aunt Candace occupied. Consequently, Estelle and I didn't have a spare moment until early afternoon, when Aunt Adelaide finally came out of the back room and took over at the front desk.

"Sorry I took so long," my aunt told me. "I haven't submitted the paperwork yet, but it's mostly done. *No* thanks to you, Candace… Why did you decide to list a self-cleaning whiteboard as a business expense?"

Aunt Candace looked scandalised. "It's a necessary purchase!"

"Not for the library," Aunt Adelaide said firmly. "Have you made any progress with that translation?"

"I've managed to switch it into a third code," she said. "I haven't figured out how to turn it into one I can read yet, but the good news is that I'm no longer purple."

Aunt Adelaide made a soft noise of disbelief. "Purple? You're lucky that's all it did to you. A third code, you say?"

"Are all these codes of Grandma's creation?" I asked, curious despite myself. "Or does the spell make them up as it goes along?"

"I haven't a clue," said Aunt Adelaide. "Candace, where —?" She broke off when Aunt Candace sped off and vanished into the reference section.

"Where's she off to?" Estelle stepped into view, looking somewhat frazzled. "She's running as if Cass's manticore is on her tail."

"I assume she had an idea," I said. "Or another 'emergency,' but this time, she didn't turn purple."

Aunt Adelaide tutted. "If she's going to the language division, I doubt there's anything in there that wouldn't have already worked on your father's journal, Rory."

"At least she gave it back without turning the pages purple." I patted my coat pocket. "She didn't give me back the translation spell yet, but I won't have time to use that for a while."

"Why… because of the professor?" Aunt Adelaide looked between Estelle and me. "What happened earlier? I didn't have time to ask."

Estelle and I quickly filled her in on everything she'd missed, including our visit to campus and our conversations with Professor Quinn and then Jesse Rogan.

"You really think his death wasn't an accident?" Aunt Adelaide asked. "Surely, Edwin would be investigating if he believed the same."

"You know what he's like about us getting involved in matters that are supposed to be up to the police," said Estelle. "Nobody called the police from campus, either, but the two witnesses didn't have the professor's best interests at heart. I knew him, Mum. It makes no sense for him to drop dead out of nowhere, and I don't believe it was a simple lab accident either."

"You want to talk to Edwin?" Aunt Adelaide guessed.

"We can both go," I added. "I haven't heard from Xavier today, but he's the one who collected the professor's soul and saw the scene for himself. Edwin might not listen to us, but he's more likely to believe the Reaper."

"He really ought to trust your word by now," my aunt

said. "You can go—and Rory, I'll make sure my sister gives back your translation spell."

"Thanks." I smiled in gratitude, though in truth, I didn't mind Aunt Candace borrowing the spell for the time being if it kept her from getting too deeply involved in our quest to learn the truth about the professor's death. I did wonder if that spell Jesse Rogan had paraded around campus was of the same sort as the translation spell, but I'd decided not to mention it in front of Aunt Candace in case it gave her any ideas.

Leaving Aunt Adelaide at the front desk, Estelle and I walked outside into a grey, drizzly day. I shivered, pulling up the hood of my coat. "Want to fetch Xavier on the way? I can't promise his boss will let him come with us..."

"With luck, Edwin will believe us without needing Xavier's confirmation." Estelle pulled up her own hood. "I think I'll pass on visiting the Grim Reaper."

"I don't blame you for that." I hoped Xavier's boss hadn't reprimanded him for sharing details of the murder scene with us—and it *was* a murder scene, I was sure—but I sent him a text message anyway. "I'm not so sure about Edwin, though. This time, nobody thinks Professor Booker's death was suspicious except for the two of us."

"Well, this isn't the first time Xavier's accidentally stumbled upon a murder scene while collecting a soul," she commented. "I expect Edwin will be slow to believe us, but if it comes to it, even he can't deny the word of the Reaper."

We walked down the narrow street alongside the clock tower and out onto the walkway that ran parallel to the beach. A short pier jutted out into the sea, and various stalls selling ice cream and snacks had popped up around the area. Given the drizzle, not many people were outside, or at least, not without wearing raincoats.

Edwin watched us enter the police station through the

automatic doors with a hint of the long-suffering expression he usually wore when dealing with our family, though it was less pronounced than it would have been if we'd brought Aunt Candace.

"Hey, Edwin," said Estelle. "Sorry to bother you, but—but I think someone might have been murdered on campus yesterday."

The elf policeman's brows shot up into his thinning hairline. "Murdered? I assume you're referring to that professor —Booker, is it?"

"You heard, then?" Estelle pushed down her hood, scattering raindrops over the floor. "He died in a lab—a lab he shouldn't have even been in—under suspicious circumstances."

"It's always your family, isn't it?" His jaw twitched. "Professor Booker died in a lab accident, as far as the reports go. Nobody has called the police from the campus, and you weren't there yourself, were you?"

"Charles Booker was my mentor." Estelle's voice wavered a little. "I know him, and I know there's no good reason for him to have been in that lab. He wasn't an alchemist. Did you know that some kind of potion was spilled at the crime scene?"

"Nobody said anything about a crime scene," Edwin said. "From what I've heard from the paramedics' first impressions, he seems to have accidentally ingested a deadly herb... an accident, I'm sure, since nobody else was in the room at the time, and he had traces of the substance on his fingers as well."

"What about the student who found him?" Estelle's voice still wavered, but she pushed on. "Jesse Rogan, who was expelled earlier this year for plagiarism by Professor Booker himself. He shouldn't have been on campus, since he got kicked out months ago, and we caught him making mischief there earlier."

"Jesse Rogan?" Edwin repeated. "I haven't had any reports from the university, and if I went after every student who caused trouble on campus, I'd never leave the place."

Evidently, nobody had reported Jesse's trespassing to the police… yet. "Xavier fetched the professor's soul," I said. "He shares our suspicions."

He hadn't replied to my message yet, but the graveyard wasn't known for having a reliable phone signal.

"The Reaper." Edwin shook his head. "It's his job to ferry souls, not identify what counts as a crime scene and what doesn't."

"You've taken his word as evidence before." The trouble was that Xavier hadn't seen anything that definitively indicated the professor's death was anything other than accidental, and to say otherwise was to take a leap that the no-nonsense head of the local police force was simply unwilling to make.

"He didn't see anyone poison the professor, did he?" he queried. "If he did, that'd be evidence. If not…"

"No, but—Professor Booker wasn't meant to be in the labs." That was flimsy as far as evidence went, I knew, but it was all I had left. "Neither was Jesse, and he got expelled months ago. He also threatened Estelle when she tried to throw him off campus earlier."

"If Estelle wants to make a complaint against this Jesse Rogan for threatening her, she's welcome to, but it sounds like the campus staff ought to step up," he said. "I got a call last week from a parent threatening to prosecute the university because they kicked out a student for blowing up a lab a week ago or so."

"Oh—I heard about that one." Estelle's brow pinched. "Edwin, I don't want to cause you any hassle, but I really believe this is worth looking into. I'm talking to the other staff on campus, but none of them has the authority to open an investigation."

"Until someone brings evidence stronger than a hunch, I'm afraid there's nothing I can do," Edwin told her. "Once the full autopsy reports come in, we'll see. Now, go on, both of you. Get back to work."

"I think he's highly strung," I whispered to Estelle as we left the police station. "Honestly, I realise he can't be in multiple places at once, but he's the head of the police, isn't he? Who else has the authority to talk to the staff up on campus?"

"I know." Her expression clouded. "The problem is it's hard for me to explain to the other staff why I think Professor Booker's death was suspicious without mentioning *why* I called him an hour before he died. Maybe I should have told Edwin that..."

"He'd probably still file that into the 'not enough evidence' category." I huddled in my coat as the sea breeze blew into our faces. "Also, what was that about another student blowing up a lab?"

Estelle pulled out her phone. "I can't remember who it was, but I'll check."

She scrolled through her messages as we walked back to the town square and then swore under her breath. "Nova Lyle. That's the student's name. Doesn't that ring a bell?"

"Nova Lyle?" I was struck by the memory of a wild-haired witch who'd tried unsuccessfully to brew a love potion back in February when I'd visited campus. "Yeah. She was one of the suspects for shooting Cupid."

I could certainly see her getting expelled for blowing up a lab, but had her parents really tried to set the police on the university? I didn't know her well enough to make a judgment call—we'd only met once—but she'd spent enough time in the lab Professor Booker had died in to make me wonder if she might have some ideas. Such as what that spilled potion was.

"Weird." Estelle put her phone away. "She turned out to be innocent, didn't she?"

"As innocent as possible for someone who brewed love potions in her spare time," I replied. "What do you think? Should we check in with her?"

"I'll have to find out if Nova is still around. She might have left."

We dropped in at Zee's bakery to buy lunch and then crossed the square back to the library. There, Aunt Adelaide was helping a group of students navigate the research section as Jet watched from his perch atop the shelves. I watched the students, wondering if any of them had known the professor... or Nova Lyle. As they departed for the Reading Corner, Aunt Adelaide moved in and took the bag Estelle offered her.

"Thanks." My aunt smiled, selecting a muffin from the bag. "Did you have any luck with Edwin?"

"Nope," I replied. "He doesn't think Professor Booker's death was anything but an accident, though he said the paramedics thought he'd died from poisoning. I know it's easy for someone to accidentally get poisoned in a lab full of potions and herbs, but he wouldn't entertain any other possibilities."

Estelle held her own muffin in one hand and her phone in the other. "I've already got people watching for Jesse, and I told them to call the police if he shows up again," she said. "Even if he doesn't turn out to have had anything to do with Professor Booker's death, I figure he'll come back to cause trouble again sooner or later."

"Have you asked any of the students?" I asked. "There are some in the Reading Corner right now. They might have known him... and they might also know if Nova is still around."

"True." Estelle lowered her phone. "Yeah, that's quicker than messaging everyone I know. Thanks, Rory. I let my common sense fly out the window for a moment there."

"It happens. You're under a lot of stress." I finished my muffin while Estelle went to the Reading Corner at the back of the library.

"She *is* under stress," Aunt Adelaide agreed. "I'm glad you're looking out for her. You know Estelle. She tends to take too much on herself."

"Pity Cass didn't inherit some of that," I commented. "She only applies her sense of responsibility to cleaning out manticore cages."

"I think she misses Sylvester."

"Huh?" I screwed up my muffin wrapper and tossed it into the bin. "Misses him? He's still here… somewhere."

"Exactly." Aunt Adelaide's mouth turned down at the corners. "The two used to spend a lot of time together, but ever since that door reappeared, Sylvester's been avoiding the third floor like the plague."

"You'd think him not being there would encourage her to come downstairs more often, not less."

"No… well, Cass wouldn't want to leave her animals, would she?"

"I guess not." It was hard to tell with my cousin; while she was less unfriendly towards me than she'd been when I'd initially moved to the library—or even towards Laney, to whom she'd been outright hostile—she wasn't inclined to ask for a shoulder to lean on when compared to her sister. Talking to Cass was rather like handling a baby dragon. I never knew if I was going to get my fingers bitten off.

Estelle returned from the back of the library, looking preoccupied. "Turns out she *is* still on campus."

"Who, Nova?"

Estelle inclined her head. "She paid for accommodation for the term, and she hasn't gone home yet."

"And… you want to talk to her?" Someone who spent as much time in the lab as Nova did might have some insight, but Estelle's cagey manner suggested that wasn't all she'd learned from the students. "What else?"

She drew in a breath. "Professor Booker was the one who kicked her out."

"For blowing up a lab?"

"Apparently so," she said. "According to some of the students, he flipped out on her and instantly expelled her."

My heart skipped a beat. "Harsh."

"Yes, and it doesn't sound like him." Estelle looked down at her phone in her hand. "Two people have confirmed it was him, though. I really didn't know what to think, so I figured talking to Nova herself would help."

"You're not going to speak to a possible murderer alone, are you?" Aunt Adelaide said, overhearing. "If you go back to campus, take Sylvester with you."

"Is he even around?" I hadn't seen the owl all day, which wasn't that unusual, given his new reluctance to enter the upper corridor. "I'll go with Estelle instead. I don't mind."

She sucked in a breath. "Then take your own familiar, Rory. He can fly back here for help if you run into trouble."

"All right—Jet?"

My familiar came swooping down in a cloud of black wings. "Here, partner!"

"We're off to campus," I told him. "You can stretch your wings for a bit."

"If Nova ends up being the killer, she's not going to attack us in the middle of the day," Estelle told Aunt Adelaide. "I don't believe in taking unnecessary risks, but Nova will be moving back home from campus any day now. This might be our only chance to speak to her."

Aunt Adelaide gave a hesitant nod. "All right, but be careful."

Once again, Estelle and I left the library and walked across the square to the high street, hoods pulled up and both metaphorical and literal clouds hovering over our heads. Above the campus, the sky was a moody light grey smudged with darker black and grey like a painter's palette.

This time, Estelle veered towards the west side of campus, where the student accommodation was located. Brick tower blocks occupied the space, and she asked a passing student for directions before entering one of the buildings. We climbed a staircase to the first floor, and halfway up, we encountered a life-sized inflatable manticore that sent Jet flying upward with a shriek of alarm.

"It's not real, Jet," I told him. "Unlike Cass's. You know she offered to set him loose here on campus?"

"I hope you said no." Estelle sidestepped the inflatable manticore.

"Obviously, but I thought it'd be one way to get rid of Jesse."

She snorted. "You aren't wrong. Also, I'm not sure which flat is Nova's, but if she's as prone to explosions as she is in the lab, her room won't be hard to find."

A singed smell greeted us upon entering the first-floor corridor, and Estelle stopped at a door that was patched with craggy lines, as if it had been repaired with a shoddy repair spell at least twice. The door creaked alarmingly when Estelle knocked and nearly fell off its hinges when Nova answered.

Given the stack of boxes behind her, Nova was clearly making a half-hearted effort at packing. That, or she hadn't bothered to unpack properly to begin with. Her wild dark hair curled to her shoulders, and the ends were slightly singed.

"What…?" Her brow furrowed as she took us in. "What're you doing here? You're Estelle, right? And you, you're the newer librarian who was looking for who shot Cupid a few months back."

"That's right," Estelle said. "Are you moving out this week?"

"Soon." Her shoulders slumped. "It's unfair, you know. I should have been given a chance."

"You blew up a lab, right?" I asked. "Did anyone get hurt?"

"A miscalculation," she said. "Yeah, Professor Booker got caught in the blast, but I apologised, and it wasn't my fault I didn't realise he was there."

"You know he's dead, right?" Estelle asked.

"Yeah." Her gaze darkened. "What? It wasn't me. I haven't been allowed into the labs since."

She might be telling the truth, but it was difficult to know for sure. "Didn't your parents threaten the university?"

She groaned. "Yeah… my mum flipped out when I told her I was expelled. I told her not to cause a fuss, but she ignored me."

"Has she ever been on campus herself?" asked Estelle.

"Definitely not," Nova replied. "She and my dad live on the other side of the country. They rarely come and visit."

I scraped the back of my mind for any other possible questions. "Do you know why the professor was in the alchemy lab to begin with? It doesn't seem like his area…"

"It isn't." She gave a wry smile. "I can guess, though. I bet he was meeting that Professor Quinn."

"Professor Quinn?" Estelle echoed. "She works in the same department as him. Why would she need to go there?"

"They were having an affair, of course," she said. "Professor Quinn is married. They didn't want anyone to know, and hardly anyone uses that lab. I told them I'd keep their secret, but it didn't do any good in the end."

Estelle's eyes widened; plainly, this was news to her too. "Is she around?"

Nova shrugged. "No clue, sorry."

Professor Quinn had been here yesterday, though... and we seemed to have another possible suspect to add to the list.

6

Professor Quinn wasn't on campus, as we learned when Estelle walked straight from the student accommodation to the theory building and returned with a downcast expression on her face. "She's left. Hasn't been seen since yesterday."

I raised a brow. "Guilty conscience?"

"No—no, I don't see her as a potential murderer. She was really upset yesterday, remember?" Estelle hunched her shoulders and began walking back towards the gate. "She's probably taken a couple of days off to get her head together. No surprise, given how close the two of them were. *How* did I not see it?"

"It sounds like they were taking great pains to hide their affair from everyone around them." I walked alongside her, Jet flying overhead. "I thought she was acting odd yesterday, but I figured she was just shaken by Professor Booker's death."

"That was what I thought too," Estelle said. "And I have no excuse, given that I've spent a lot longer in that department, and I knew—well, I didn't know Professor Quinn personally, but we ran into one another a lot."

"I guess you knew she was married?" Awkward.

"Yes—which explains why she's lying low, but she'll be back for the funeral, I expect," Estelle replied. "I guess we also know why she was so interested in getting into his office yesterday."

"No kidding."

We walked back down the high street in a pensive silence. Over the square towered the library, a blocky yet elegant shape etched against the moody grey sky, and my thoughts came back to earth as we climbed the steps to the entrance. Jet flew in ahead of us, and Aunt Adelaide greeted us at the desk.

"That didn't take long," she said. "No trouble?"

"We did learn some things, but Nova Lyle doesn't strike me as the professor's killer," I explained. "And she said her parents lived on the other side of the country, and they were the ones who threatened to call the police on the university, which makes it kinda unlikely that they came here to commit murder."

"That was what I was thinking," Estelle said. "Professor Booker expelled her in a fit of anger when she blew up the lab on him, but I'd say Jesse has more of a temperament for murder than Nova does."

"He did?" Aunt Adelaide studied us. "Was the professor usually prone to inflicting harsh punishments?"

"No—which made this one unusual," Estelle said quietly. "We also found out that he was having an affair with Professor Quinn, and they used to meet up in the labs."

My aunt's lips compressed. "Professor Quinn?"

"Another professor in the same department," Estelle clarified. "She was married, and—she's also not on campus right now, so we couldn't talk to her ourselves. She seemed really upset yesterday, so it's unlikely that she was the one who killed him, but—well, it explains why he was in the lab before he died."

"Not why he had a spilled potion on the floor next to him, though," I added. "Unless it was one of Nova's love potions."

Estelle snorted and then pressed her hand to her forehead. "How is this getting *more* complicated with every passing moment? It shouldn't be any of my business who the professor wanted to spend his time with."

"Estelle, you don't have to do this." Aunt Adelaide studied her daughter with a worried frown. "I know you cared for the professor a lot, but he wouldn't have wanted you to potentially risk your life for his sake."

"Who else will?" Estelle said distractedly, pacing past the desk. "Edwin won't. He thinks our family is making trouble again, and I can see why he'd assume a lab accident was the likelier explanation. Frankly, I'd rather believe that myself, but…"

Aunt Adelaide moved to put an arm around her daughter. "None of this is your fault."

"I didn't say it was." Estelle rubbed the back of her hand over her eyes. "But I'm the one in charge of cleaning up the mess he left behind—and that isn't even counting the funeral. Professor Quinn will be back by then, I'm sure, but—" Her phone began to buzz. "Not again."

Estelle ducked out from under her mother's arm and crossed the lobby to the living quarters while Aunt Adelaide watched her with her brow creased.

"I don't get the impression anyone else on campus believes her," I said quietly. "About his death not being an accident, I mean."

Aunt Adelaide sucked in a breath. "Yes, it sounds like this professor had a very complicated life, and I don't know that we can do anything more to convince Edwin that his death was out of the ordinary. Those university labs can be lethal on a good day."

"True," I said. "If Professor Booker was spending a lot of time in there, it explains why he was found in a department he didn't work in, but I didn't hear anything about Professor Quinn being there as well. It sounds like only Jesse Rogan and Dr Hayes saw his body."

"Dr Hayes?"

"She works in the labs," I explained. "She was the person Jesse reported to when he found the body, assuming he didn't put it there himself. Dr Hayes... she also didn't seem to like him much."

"Who, Jesse?"

"Professor Booker," I clarified. "I know, it's complicated, but I'm not leaving Estelle to bear the burden of this alone."

"You're a good friend to her, Rory," said Aunt Adelaide. "I don't want you risking your life either, though. The university campus can be a source of trouble... though I suppose I might say the same of the library. Places where knowledge is gathered have that tendency."

"That's true." The library was why Estelle had called Professor Booker that day in the first place, and I knew it must be weighing heavily on her mind, contributing to her sense of responsibility towards him. Yet it wouldn't do to dwell on the unchangeable, so I sought a change of subject. "Have you submitted the tax forms yet?"

"Not yet," she replied. "The internet was down earlier, and then you and Estelle were out."

"I'll watch the desk while you finish," I offered. "Jet and I don't mind. It's quiet enough in here."

Aunt Candace, as was typical, had vanished upstairs, but not many people were down on the lower levels. Aunt Adelaide scanned the area and smiled. "Thank you, Rory. I have to admit, I'm struggling to remember how we coped without you here."

Her words warmed me to my core, washing away some of my lingering doubts. In a few months, a year would have passed since I'd moved here, and while my old life was a distant memory, it was rare that I got the chance to stop and reflect on how much progress I'd made in a relatively short time.

Estelle was a major part in making it easy for me to transition to life in the magical world. Leaving her to investigate Professor Booker's murder alone would be a poor way to repay her.

Shortly after Aunt Adelaide left for the back room, a message from Xavier came through saying the Grim Reaper had dragged him off on some errand and that he'd drop by later. When someone knocked on the library door a minute later, I thought at first that Xavier's boss had let him go early after all.

I was mistaken. The door swung open, framing the formidable presence of Evangeline, leader of the local vampires. She didn't look in the least like she'd walked here in the rain; not so much as a droplet of water clung to her luscious curls, while her face would make supermodels faint in envy. My heart leapt into my throat when she bared her pointed teeth at me in a smile.

"Erm… what are you doing here?" It wasn't late enough for Laney to be awake yet, so Evangeline hadn't come to see her. No… she'd come to seek *me* out.

"I thought we could have a talk," she said. "Is that acceptable, Aurora?"

She didn't expect me to say no, surely. "Yes… what is it?"

I genuinely had no clue what she could possibly want with me. Evangeline had no ties to the university, so the professor's death would hold no interest for her, and she'd waited far too long to have urgent questions about the newly rediscovered upstairs corridor. Yes, she did have an overt interest in my dad's journal, but it'd been weeks since she'd last mentioned the subject. When her gaze lingered on my face a little too long, I focused on the desk so that she wouldn't pluck any thoughts out of my mind without my permission.

"I heard that a certain individual is back in town," she said softly.

"What—who?" *Not one of the Founders?* No—she'd have told me sooner if that was the case. All the same, my entire body tensed. "Which individual?"

"The one who gave you the book that you acquired from the Founders."

The book? Hang on. "Professor Colt."

"Correct."

Professor Colt was back in town? "His former colleague died. That is why he came back, I assume. For the funeral."

"Are you quite sure about that?" she asked. "I gathered from delving into the minds of a few people around the university campus that he's been back more than once in the past few weeks."

My mouth parted. She'd been on campus, poking into people's minds? "I don't know why you're telling me this. Why would you be interested in what goes on at the university?"

Unless she thought Professor Colt had been involved in his colleague's death? *Or... wait. Professor Colt was interested in knowledge the Founders wanted. Does that mean Professor Booker was too?*

"I find it a useful exercise to watch those who come and go from campus," she said. "After all, the university is the main source of new visitors to Ivory Beach, aside from tourists—and one of the biggest sources of trouble, except perhaps for your library."

Did she know my aunt had made the same comment earlier? That was doubtful. Everyone knew of the library's propensity to attract trouble.

"That still doesn't explain why you thought I'd urgently want to know Professor Colt was in town," I pointed out. "Unless you think *he's* the one who got Professor Booker killed."

"I don't recall mentioning that name."

"You know he's dead if you've been to campus," I said, undeterred by her feigned ignorance. "Do you know if anyone else over there suspects his death wasn't an accident?"

"I know nothing of this other professor," said Evangeline. "I simply felt compelled to see if the man your father entrusted with that valuable book had paid you a visit."

"Why would he come into the library after everything he went through to get rid of that book?" Professor Colt had been so afraid of the consequences for keeping a book the Founders wanted that he'd been willing to hand it over to the Grim Reaper, of all people. While the book had ultimately ended up in the library, the Founders hadn't come back for it—yet. "Is this to do with the Founders? Is that what you're implying? Wait—you had Laney looking for them, didn't you?"

"I have several locations I've been watching for a while," she said. "Nothing has come of my search thus far, but I hoped the professor might have insight."

Why not ask him yourself? Admittedly, Evangeline scared the living daylights out of most people, including me, and if she approached Professor Colt herself, he might leave the country this time around.

"I see that you know nothing, so I shall bid you farewell for now, Aurora." And she vanished out of the door before I could utter another word.

I was still gaping after her when Xavier appeared on the doorstep several moments later. "Hey, Rory. Was that Evangeline I just saw?"

"She knew you were coming and ran off," I guessed. "Dammit. I should have asked her to stop sending Laney into danger while she was here. Not that she ever listens to me, but still."

"Was that why she came here?" he asked. "Laney isn't awake yet, is she?"

"No, but Professor Colt is back in town."

"Is he?" Xavier closed the door behind him. "Since when?"

"Weeks ago, Evangeline said." I glanced over my shoulder, my skin prickling, but nobody was around except for Jet, who perched snoozing on a nearby shelf. "Bloody vampires. They can't give a straight answer."

"Seems to be a personality trait," he agreed. "Sorry I took so long to reply to your message. It's taken me this long to escape my boss. How'd it go with Edwin earlier?"

"Badly." I filled him in on everything we'd learned that morning, including what happened during our two visits to campus.

"I might not have helped matters if I'd come with you to the police station," Xavier said. "I might have escorted the professor's soul into the afterlife, but I don't have conclusive proof that his death wasn't an accident."

"I guess your boss wouldn't be a fan of the idea either."

"He isn't even a fan of me breathing. Says it makes me seem too human."

I laughed in disbelief. "Seriously?"

"Yes, unfortunately," said Xavier. "As for the professor… if he *was* murdered, it sounds as if there's a long list of possible culprits."

"And we can add one more now Evangeline has decided to let me know that Professor Colt is back in town."

"You think the professor was involved in his colleague's death?"

"Not directly, I don't think, but I don't know if she thinks the Founders might follow him."

"Might they?" Tension underlay his voice. "I can look for the professor myself if you want to talk to him."

"I don't *want* to, but I'll see what Estelle thinks of the idea first. She'll want to know too."

Ignoring a suggestion from the vampires' leader, however dubious her motives, usually wasn't a good idea, but we had quite enough people on our suspect list already. I went to the living quarters and found Estelle lying on the sofa, her arm angled over her face and her phone still clutched in her fist.

"Estelle?" I peered at her face. "Are you asleep?"

"No, I needed a lie-down." She lifted her head. "Oh—hi, Xavier. Is my mum watching the desk?"

"No, she's submitting the tax forms. I thought you were on the phone."

"I was until a minute ago." She rose to a sitting position. "Sorry."

"It's not your fault everyone wants you to answer to them," I replied. "Anyway—I wondered if you heard Evangeline. She just dropped by a minute ago."

"What?" She ran a hand over her forehead. "She must have been fast. I didn't hear her… not that I was listening."

"She told me that Professor Colt was back in town," I explained. "I'm not clear on why she was so keen for me to know, except that he may have talked to Professor Booker before his death."

Estelle paled. "What—does she think he was involved himself?"

"I haven't a clue," I replied. "But I thought Professor Colt left town out of fear for his life and he was happy to have that book off his hands. Why come back?"

"I don't get it either." Her head dropped to her chest. "They *were* in the same department, so I can understand Professor Colt coming back for the funeral, but why on earth would Evangeline be interested?"

"I don't know," I replied. "She's been poking into people's minds on campus and found out the professor's been back in town for longer than a few days, though."

"Nobody mentioned him on the phone." Estelle ran a hand through her tangled curls. "I heard Professor Quinn took a couple of days off, so at least we know she's in town, if not on campus. I don't know about Professor Colt, though."

Hmm. I was inclined to place Professor Quinn lower on the suspect list than some of the others, and it made sense that she'd want to avoid campus for the time being. Maybe she hadn't wanted to deal with her colleagues' questions, whether or not they'd known of the affair between Professor Booker and herself.

Xavier cleared his throat. "I can help. If there's anything you need a Reaper for. Any locked doors you want to get through?"

"Locked doors?" Estelle echoed. "Aside from the lab, no… but do you really want to get involved in this, Xavier?"

"I'm already involved," he said. "If there's the slightest chance a certain group of vampires are behind this, I'm in."

He wasn't wrong. "I'm up for a little breaking and entering if you are."

The decision was Estelle's, though. I looked at her, and she nodded slowly. "All right."

7

The three of us set off for campus after the library closed for the evening. Aunt Adelaide had expressed doubts at the idea when we'd told her, but she'd been downright alarmed to learn of Evangeline's previous visit. For that reason, she'd agreed that it was worth another look around campus, this time in a Reaper's company.

Aunt Candace, meanwhile, hadn't emerged from wherever she'd disappeared to when a lightning bolt of inspiration hit her earlier. Probably for the best, as we already risked drawing attention with three of us present. The high street was bustling with people walking home from the office, and nobody looked twice at us, but that might change when we reached campus.

"What's the plan?" I asked Estelle in an undertone. "Start with the lab?"

"Yes, and if we don't find anything in there, Professor Quinn's office will be empty at the moment," she said. "Might be worth looking in there."

"And—Professor Colt?"

"He won't be staying on campus if he's not back permanently."

"Makes me wonder why he came back at all." That Evangeline, of all people, had been the one to tell me he was back in town bolstered my instinct that Professor Booker's death had been the result of far more than an affair and a badly timed phone call.

We entered campus and were swallowed up in the chattering crowd of students leaving their last lectures of the day, either walking back to their accommodations or through the gates to the high street. There were enough people around that nobody seemed to notice the Reaper, at least; the crowd parted slightly on either side of Xavier without anyone being entirely conscious of it.

When we veered towards the labs, however, the crowd thinned out. Estelle and I held back while Xavier used his Reaper stealth to slip into the building and have a look around.

After a few moments, he emerged and shook his head. "There's this woman patrolling the corridors. It almost looked like she was keeping both eyes open for trespassers."

"Dr Hayes." Estelle swore under her breath. "Okay, we'll go to the theory building instead. See if she eventually gets bored and goes home."

I didn't entirely blame Dr Hayes for watching the labs like a hawk after someone had shown up dead in there, but the timing was inconvenient to say the least. Estelle resignedly led the way to the theory building and entered. She approached Professor Quinn's office first.

"Locked," she murmured. "I don't know if it's worth looking in there, but if there's the slightest chance that there are clues in her office that might help us figure out who killed Professor Booker..."

"I can unlock the door from the other side," Xavier offered. "It won't take a moment."

"Okay." Estelle stood back while Xavier vanished into shadow, and an instant later, the door to Professor Quinn's office clicked open from the inside.

Xavier appeared in the doorway, an apologetic expression on his face. "I don't know if you want to lock the door again afterwards..."

"We can use magic to do that," I whispered to Estelle as we walked in. "Erm... what exactly are we looking for in here?"

"Clues." She crossed the office to the desk, which was arranged much more neatly than Professor Booker's. Most of the papers were tucked away into cabinets, and the desk contained little more than a few pens and a stack of what appeared to be unmarked essays. "Really, it's the lab we need to look around, since it's where they spent most of their time. I hope that Dr Hayes gives up and goes home soon."

"What's her issue with the professor? Do you know?" I asked as she carefully examined the papers on the desk without touching them. "Academic rivalry?"

"Pretty much, though I doubt she was thrilled at him using the labs for romantic trysts with Professor Quinn." She took a step back and scanned the room. "I can understand why they didn't meet in here or in Professor Booker's own office, though. People would talk."

"Some of them seem to have figured out they were having an affair anyway. I guess from people in the alchemy department—" Footsteps sounded outside, prompting me to slam my mouth shut. *Uh-oh.* We had zero excuses for being in here, and even if it wasn't Professor Quinn herself, we'd have to do a hell of a job justifying what we were doing in an office that was supposed to be locked.

The footsteps passed the room, but I kept my ears pricked. The noise quietened, as if the person had slowed down, and then the sound of a door clicking open came from nearby.

Estelle's eyes widened. "Did... did they just go into Professor Booker's office?"

"Sounded like it," I murmured back. "It's not Professor Quinn?"

"I'll look." Xavier vanished into the shadows and reappeared a few seconds later. "It's him. Professor Colt."

"He's in Professor Booker's office?" Abandoning caution, I strode to the door and pushed it open quietly before stepping out into the corridor.

Professor Booker's office door had already closed, and when Estelle exited the room behind me, I let her overtake Xavier and me. She had more of a reason to be here—and to ask Professor Colt why he was sneaking around a dead man's office.

With Xavier and me behind her, Estelle strode up to Professor Booker's door and pushed it inward.

Next to the desk, Professor Colt jumped violently. "Ah—Rory? Estelle? What are you doing here?"

"I work here," Estelle said. "I could ask you the same question. Didn't you leave town?"

The professor looked like he hadn't slept in a week; his already-wild grey hair stood on end at all angles, and bags underlay the wrinkles around his eyes. "I did, briefly, but I'm still on leave from my position at the university."

"Why are you in Professor Booker's office, then?" I queried. "You know he's dead, right?"

"He had some of my books," he said. "I know it's not ideal, but I wanted them back, and I..."

"What books?" Estelle folded her arms. "Go on. Get them."

For a moment, he didn't move, his gaze darting around. "No—never mind. If it bothers you, I'll come back later..."

"Nice try," Estelle said. "I'm not buying it. Professor Booker was murdered, and now you show up on campus when everyone's gone home? Also, I'm told you two met with one another before his death."

"You think he was murdered?" The colour drained from his already-pasty face. "If... if he was, then I had nothing to do with it."

"I'd like to believe you," said Estelle, "but unless you give me a very good reason for your breaking into his office, I'm going to have to assume the worst."

"You've got it wrong," he mumbled. "I'm no killer."

"I thought you were terrified of the Founders finding you," I said. "Now you show up here after dark and start poking through the office of a man who might have been killed by the Founders themselves, and you expect us not to be suspicious?"

"He wasn't—" He broke off. "Dammit. Why didn't he listen to me?"

"What does that mean?" said Estelle.

"I told him not to draw their attention." A hint of despair underlay his voice. "I thought he knew enough to be careful."

"Draw their attention how?" I asked. "What exactly was he doing?"

He gave a helpless shrug. "I don't know. We've only met briefly to talk about changes on campus since I left town, nothing else."

"I don't think I believe you," Estelle said in an uncharacteristically sharp tone. "Why exactly did you feel the need to tell Professor Booker to be careful if you didn't think he was in danger? You can't deny it's suspicious that he shows up dead, and then it turns out he's been in contact with someone who left town to flee the Founders. And now that same person is sneaking around his office after hours the day after he died."

"He was poisoned, which doesn't sound like the Founders." He took in a shaky breath. "I know it looks suspicious that I'm here, but I can promise that I'm not the person who killed Charles. I want to know the full story as much as you do."

Hmm. He was right that the Founders didn't need to resort to poisoning when they had more-efficient ways of getting rid of their targets. "They might have poisoned him to divert the blame from themselves."

"No." He shook his head. "The Founders kill to make a point. They wouldn't disguise one of their murders as an accident—and you know, it *does* appear like an accident. I rather hoped I might find a clue that would hint otherwise, but I haven't been able to get into the labs yet."

"Is Dr Hayes still there?" Estelle's voice dropped to a whisper when the sound of more footsteps came from outside. "Did you bring anyone with you?"

"No... no." He shook his head. "I came alone..."

A voice rang through the corridor. "Who has been in my office?"

"Crap," Estelle said in a hushed voice. "That's Professor Quinn. I forgot to close the door."

Uh-oh. *She's back?* "I thought she was on leave."

"Apparently not." Estelle remained still for a moment, and then she squared her shoulders and walked out of the room.

I hesitated, not wanting to turn my back on Professor Colt in case he made a run for it—but Xavier stepped into his path.

"I'll watch him, Rory," he whispered. "You should back up Estelle."

"All right." I pushed open the door as Professor Quinn drew in a sharp breath.

"Estelle," she said. "What are you doing here?"

"Professor Quinn," she said. "Sorry… I was looking for some of the professor's seminar students' essays, and I thought you might have them."

Tension underlay Professor Quinn's reply. "Why on earth would you think I'd have anything of his?"

"Because the two of you were close." Estelle inhaled. "I'm not judging, Professor, but some of us guessed what was going on between you."

A tense moment passed while I lingered in the doorway, not wanting to intrude but unable to retreat into Professor Booker's office without making a noise and giving away my presence.

Professor Quinn finally replied in a shaky voice, "I have no idea what you're talking about."

"I haven't told anyone else. Don't worry," Estelle said. "Look, I'm not here to pass judgement on you. I just wanted to know about Professor Booker… and if he was doing anything that might have endangered his life."

Conscious of Professor Colt in the room behind me, I stepped fully outside, letting the door swing closed behind me. Professor Quinn hissed out a breath as Estelle cleared her throat. "Ah—Rory won't tell anyone either. She's my cousin, and she doesn't even work here, but—but I need to know the truth about the professor."

Professor Quinn had gone pale, and her mouth parted. "What do you mean 'endangered his life'?"

"Charles Booker was murdered," Estelle said. "I have reason to believe he drew the attention of a certain group of very dangerous vampires. You might know them—the Founders."

Professor Quinn made a choked noise. "I don't know what you're talking about. Charles was an academic, not engaged in risky pursuits—and besides, it's absurd to suggest there might be *vampires* hiding on campus."

"Charles was poisoned to death," Estelle said, "which suggests his killer was human... but that doesn't rule out a connection with the vampires nonetheless. I need to know what you know, Professor Quinn, if we want to stop the same from happening to anyone else."

"I haven't the faintest clue," she said. "Really. I didn't have anything to do with this."

"What about your husband?" Professor Colt walked out of the office behind me, followed by a swift-footed Xavier.

Professor Quinn gasped, and Estelle winced at the other professor's words.

"Don't bring him into this." Professor Quinn's voice trembled when she looked upon her former colleague. "He doesn't know, and now he never will—as long as you hold your tongue."

Professor Colt surveyed her. "I'll keep your secret, but you... you knew Charles better than the rest of us did. What exactly was he doing in the lab when he died?"

"Nothing to do with me," she said in a brittle tone. "What were *you* doing in Charles's office, exactly?"

"That was what we wanted to know too," Estelle answered. "We found him sneaking around there alone, but Professor Booker met with him recently. Did you meet him as well?"

"No, I most certainly did not," she said. "Also, I have more respect for Charles than to break into his office after his death, unlike this man."

"I'm here for answers," Professor Colt said. "Charles and I were friends. Perhaps not as close as you two, but you must know his death was no accident."

"It's not my doing," Professor Quinn said. "I told you I'm

not involved. I... I don't know who killed him. It certainly wasn't my husband either."

"I never thought it was." Professor Colt grimaced. "I had to ask. I know you've been avoiding campus recently..."

"Of course, I have," Professor Quinn replied in uneven tones. "I can't even mourn Charles without drawing suspicion, much less sneak around his office after hours."

"If I'm to believe that neither of you was involved in his death," Estelle said, "you still know enough between the two of you to make an educated guess about who might have had reason to harm him. Aside from the Founders, he recently expelled two students, didn't he?"

"Who—Jesse Rogan?" Professor Quinn's eyebrows shot up. "You think this was an act of revenge?"

"I don't know what to think," Estelle said, "but Jesse was the person who found Professor Booker's body, wasn't he?"

"You think he poisoned Charles?" Professor Quinn asked. "Is that more likely than an accident?"

"He wasn't supposed to be on campus in the first place," Estelle said. "As for the professor... was he waiting for you, Professor Quinn?"

She shook her head. "No... no, we hadn't arranged to meet during the day. I don't know why he was there."

Wait, he *hadn't* been waiting for her? Why else would he have been in the lab?

"He didn't work in that department... unless he was meeting someone else?" Estelle's gaze flickered over to Professor Colt, who also shook his head.

"I wasn't here myself at the time," he said. "I *did* know Jesse Rogan when I taught here, and the boy's certainly lacking in morals. What did he get expelled for?"

"Plagiarism," Estelle replied. "That was back in June, but we found him on campus this week, trying to convince the students to hire him to help them cheat on their assignments.

I don't trust him an inch, and as soon as I heard he was the one who found Charles's body, I had to wonder if he was the one who put him there."

"What's this about vampires, then?" Professor Quinn said. "Who's to say anyone else was involved?"

Evangeline. Not that I wanted to bring her up in front of Professor Quinn when I didn't entirely trust that she was telling the truth. Professor Colt, though… "Professor Colt here fled the town to avoid the Founders. Now he's back and someone's dead, so I had to ask."

"It's not them," Professor Colt said firmly. "Did you report Jesse to the authorities?"

"We talked to the police," Estelle said. "But they wanted more proof the professor's death wasn't an accident, and we don't have the knowledge to make that call. Unless either of you wants to help?"

Professor Quinn grimaced. "I would prefer to keep our affair quiet."

"And *I* would prefer to keep a low profile for my own safety," Professor Colt said, "not merely to save face."

"Hey, that's enough," said Estelle when Professor Quinn let out an angry huff at her former colleague's comment. "You both knew Charles best. Would you let his murderer go unpunished for your own selfish reasons?"

"I have no proof to offer the police either," Professor Quinn said. "If Charles was involved in anything dangerous, he didn't tell me."

"And I made my own stance clear," added Professor Colt.

"Except when you sneaked into his office," I couldn't help adding.

A flush crept over his face. "That's hardly evidence, is it?"

"Depends." Estelle's gaze flickered to Professor Quinn. "This is ridiculous. *One* of you has to be willing to help us."

Professor Colt shook his head, his shoulders hunching. "I wish I could."

Professor Quinn hesitated. "I'll ask my colleagues about whether they saw Jesse on campus recently, but I can't say it'll help prove Charles's death was no accident."

"What about Dr Hayes?" I thought back to her appearance in the labs. "She works in the alchemy department, and she's the one Jesse went to when he found the body."

"Dr Hayes?" Professor Quinn blanched. "You think I should ask for *her* help?"

"She's a witness… or as close as possible, aside from Jesse," Estelle said. "She's not my biggest fan, either, but it's safe to say she was aware of your affair."

"She'd ruin me," Professor Quinn said. "Without a doubt."

"I doubt she wants anyone running around campus committing murder any more than you do." I had some sympathy for Professor Quinn, but asking Dr Hayes for help was hardly as scary as making a request of the head of the vampires or the Grim Reaper, and I'd asked a favour from both.

"Think about it," Estelle said. "We can talk to her first, after we look around the labs."

"Good luck with that," Professor Quinn said. "Dr Hayes has started locking the building up after dark, no doubt to deter any future breaking and entering."

Ah. That explained why she'd been patrolling the corridors earlier.

Estelle exhaled in a sigh. "Fine, we'll come back tomorrow. Will you be here?"

"Yes," Professor Quinn said with reluctance. "I will be, and please don't break into my office again."

She ducked back into the room, leaving us alone with the professor—and Xavier, who stood behind him, preventing him from fleeing.

"Will *you* be back here tomorrow?" I asked Professor Colt. "Because we'd like to talk to you alone."

"Not here," he said. "In fact, I'm starting to think returning to Ivory Beach at all was a mistake on my part. If *they're* in the area..."

Estelle drew in another breath. "Whether they are or not, we need to convince Edwin to investigate this as a murder, and you're one of the few people who might be able to help. We don't have to meet on campus."

"Outside," he said firmly. "In the open."

"We'll meet on the pier at noon tomorrow," Estelle suggested. "How's that sound?"

"I'll do my best to be there." He stepped back, and when Xavier moved out of the way, Professor Colt vanished into the night like a ghost.

"That sounds like he's about to do a runner," I whispered to the others. "Or sneak back into Professor Booker's office."

"He's welcome to try." Estelle pointed her wand at Professor Booker's office door and cast a locking spell. "I don't think there's anything incriminating in there, but I also don't think Professor Colt was being truthful."

"Maybe he'll be willing to talk more freely when we're off campus." I followed Xavier out of the building, Estelle on my heels. "He must want to know the truth about his colleague's death, surely, however much he might fear for his own life."

"I agree," Xavier said. "Do you want to go back to the labs?"

"Not if Dr Hayes is there," I said. "We're better off heading home... Do you want to grab something to eat on the way back? Or would you rather come to dinner at the library?"

"I'd love to," he said with a smile that improved my mood immeasurably. "Will your family mind?"

"Nah, Aunt Candace is in one of those moods where she isn't paying any attention to the real world," I said. "And Cass is... well, the last I saw of her, she was cleaning out her manticore's cage. She also offered to set him on the vampires."

"Scary." He slid his hand into mine, and my nerves began to loosen as we walked through the darkening street.

The sun sank below the horizon and rendered the library a stark towering block against the orange-tinged sky. As we reached the door, Laney stepped out into the night, the sunset painting lights onto her pale skin.

"Oh—hey, Rory." Her gaze travelled over us. "Hey, Xavier. And, Estelle. Where've you three all been?"

"Campus," I replied. "Is Evangeline sending you on another errand? Please tell me she isn't."

"Not this time," she said. "I was going for a walk. It's a nice evening."

I inhaled. "Evangeline visited the library earlier."

"Did she?" She arched a brow. "Not to pay me a visit, I take it?"

"No... she was here to give me a warning," I said. "I can explain over dinner, if you don't mind joining us?"

"Dinner with a vampire *and* a Reaper?" Her eyes gleamed with amusement. "Your aunt will have no shortage of stories to write about with this one."

8

As it turned out, Aunt Candace scarcely paid any attention to our guests. She said little, devouring her food with gusto, her enchanted pen scribbling away on the notebook at her side. Aunt Adelaide didn't try to drag her or Cass into the conversation. Fortunately, my cousin no longer smelled of manticore dung, though she seemed downright baffled by Laney's presence here, as if she'd forgotten she lived in the library altogether.

While my aunt was cooking, I'd told Laney all about Evangeline's unexpected visit as well as our various excursions to the campus, though we'd dropped the subject at the dinner table at Aunt Adelaide's request. We'd end up talking in circles anyway; none of us had reached any new conclusions about the professor's killer aside from the obvious. We'd have to see what Professor Colt said tomorrow and if he offered any new insights.

Aunt Candace was on her best behaviour until dessert, at which point she finally seemed to notice Xavier and Laney were present. "I never thought I'd see a Reaper and a vampire dine at the same table."

"We've been here for nearly an hour," Laney said mildly. "You seem distracted. Is it about that code you're working on?"

"I'll thank you to stay out of my thoughts, young lady."

"I'm not going near your thoughts. Rory told me."

When Aunt Candace levelled me with an accusing look, I shrugged. "I didn't think you'd mind me telling them. What was that idea you had earlier? When you ran off?"

"Oh, a dead end."

"That's it?" Cass looked up from her plate. "Then where've you been all day? You weren't on the third floor."

"I was perusing the language section of the library," Aunt Candace announced. "It's all very fascinating, but none of the books contained what I needed."

"You thought the code might be related to an existing language?" I guessed.

"No," she said. "I thought the *spell* might be related to one that someone might have used in the past to hide something they didn't want anyone to read. One particularly ingenious wizard translated all his documents into Trollish, did you know?"

She addressed Xavier, who blinked. "No… I can't say I did."

"Utterly incomprehensible to anyone but trolls, and everyone knows they haven't two brain cells to rub together." She snickered. "The wizard never did manage to change them back, you know. I heard he died in poverty."

"Poor guy," Estelle commented, helping herself to a trifle from the bowl Aunt Adelaide had put on the table. "You didn't find anything applicable to your situation, then?"

"No," she said. "I need something a little more *academic.*"

Estelle and I glanced at one another across the table, a hint of alarm in her gaze. *Please say she isn't going to invite herself to the university.*

"Not from me, I hope," Estelle said in falsely light tones. "I did my PhD in practical magic, not code-breaking."

"I'm aware of that," Aunt Candace said. "I suppose I shall have to look elsewhere."

When we'd finished eating, Laney started making motions in the direction of the door again. It was fully dark outside by now, but I didn't blame her for wanting to go out. Vampires' natural instincts urged them to become active at night, and Evangeline hadn't given her any missions this evening.

"If you walk past the campus, you'll let us know if you see anything odd, right?" I asked her. "I can't say I'm convinced the Founders were the ones who killed Professor Booker, but with Professor Colt back in town and Evangeline's suspicions..."

"The Founders wouldn't normally resort to poison when they have fangs," she said. "I'll keep an eye out for trouble, though."

"Be careful." I stood back and watched her leave, and I glimpsed Cass watching her too. An odd expression flickered across her face and disappeared a moment later, before she vanished behind the shelves.

Xavier took my arm. "Laney will be fine."

"I know, but—"

A crash sounded from the living quarters. I spun that way just as Estelle ran out into the lobby, clutching her phone. "Dr Hayes is dead. She was found in—in the lab."

For a moment, nobody spoke. My thoughts whirled, landing on Professor Colt—and Professor Quinn. "When was this? While we were there?"

"Must have been," she said, her face ashen. "It was after the lab was locked up for the night. Someone saw a light in the window, and when they went inside, they found..."

"Dr Hayes." Xavier looked between us, his eyes wide in

the darkened lobby. "I didn't sense anyone die. Not when we were on campus and not now."

"What—?" Estelle gaped at him. "How is that possible?"

"Nothing can fool a Reaper's senses, can it?" I asked Xavier, already knowing the answer.

"No, and if I hadn't picked up on her death, my boss certainly would have." His expression darkened. "I'll have to look for myself."

"Not alone." I stepped in. "Laney's out there too."

He shook his head. "That's not a good idea. What if you're accused of killing Dr Hayes yourself? You were on campus at the time..."

"So were Professor Colt and Professor Quinn," Estelle said. "A lot of other people too. Besides—she's not dead. Right?"

"If she's not dead, someone thinks she is," I said. "I'd like to know why that is."

"Yes... so would I," Xavier said grudgingly.

"I'm going," Estelle said. "I'll tell my mum first."

Unsurprisingly, Aunt Adelaide was not a fan of the idea, but when Estelle pointed out that the campus would be swarming with police and the attempted killer would be a fool to come back with so many people around, she relented. Partly, that was because Xavier promised to stay nearby, and he stuck close to my side as we followed the darkened streets back to campus.

With the fall of night, the shadows between buildings had deepened despite the lamplights that had come on at dusk, illuminating the crowd that had gathered outside the labs. More students and staff milled around the buildings, talking in hushed voices that formed a collective hum of noise. Estelle began to make her way through the crowd, but I hung back, not wanting to get in anyone's way.

Xavier leaned in close to me. "I'm going to look in the lab. I'll be right back."

He vanished amid the crowd with the stealth that only a Reaper could achieve. Or a vampire. *Wait... a vampire?*

I waited, tense, for several minutes, while the crowd hummed with speculation that I did my best to tune out. From the whispers, I gathered that Dr Hayes was not widely liked among students *or* staff but that nobody knew who'd wanted her dead. Professor Booker's name came up once or twice. Someone suggested a serial killer was bumping off professors. I moved closer to the group of students who'd made that suggestion, but they scattered with shrieks of alarm when Xavier walked through their group.

"Reaper!" someone yelped.

Oh boy. I scooted over to Xavier and took his arm. "I thought you were trying not to draw attention. What is it?"

"I was right—she's not dead," he said quietly. "I think she's been bitten by a vampire."

My heart jumped into my throat. "You know—the thought crossed my mind, but *which* vampire?"

"I don't know," he said. "I guess whoever found her body panicked and assumed she was dead. An easy mistake to make."

"I guess." Unfortunately, I didn't have the authority to declare someone dead or otherwise, and I saw no signs of the police amid the restless crowd. "Where's Edwin?"

"On his way, but the paramedics will be here sooner," he said. "Ah—there's Estelle."

I followed his gaze to the shadow of the building where Estelle stood talking to a couple of staff members. "Right... I'd better tell her."

Xavier led the way through the crowd of students, who parted around him in a flurry of hushed whispers.

When I reached Estelle, I caught her arm and spoke in a low voice. "She's not dead. Xavier said she was—bitten."

I didn't need to say the word "vampire" for her to understand my meaning. Estelle's eyes widened. "Seriously?"

"He's pretty sure," I murmured. "But we don't have the authority here."

"I'll tell them." Estelle indicated the professors she'd been speaking to. "The police will be here any minute now. They'll help clear the crowd, and then we can have a closer look."

Xavier and I remained hidden in shadow, but the rumours had already caught on, and cries of "Reaper" bounced back and forth amid the students.

"I think they're convinced I'm here to take Dr Hayes's soul," Xavier said in a low voice.

"Better that than the alternative." If word got out that a vampire might be on campus, there'd be a panicked stampede or worse. The question, again, was *which* vampire? And why?

"True, but I don't think I've ever been stared at this much," Xavier said. "My boss will have me under house arrest for a week if he finds out."

"At least nobody's soul needs collecting." I shrank farther back into the shadow of the building. "I wish Laney hadn't gone out. I mean, she can't be blamed for this, since she was in the library at the time…"

"She won't be," Xavier said with confidence. "I can look around campus for the intruder. Might stop people staring for a bit."

"All right—but watch your back."

Admittedly, a vampire wouldn't stand a chance of hurting a Reaper, but Xavier's departure brought a surge of unease, and the question of why a vampire would have attacked Dr Hayes in the first place took prominence in my mind. Why her?

"Police here!" a voice called from near the gates. "Let us through!"

Edwin didn't make much of an impression, but his giant troll guards did, and they parted the crowd with ease. The elf policeman sighed when he spied Estelle and me waiting for him near the building.

"Let me guess—one of you found the body?" he asked.

"No, and she's not dead," I said in a low voice. "She was bitten by a vampire—Xavier confirmed it himself."

His mouth parted. "The Reaper—where is he?"

"Looking for the intruder," I replied. "He's unlikely to be mistaken about whether or not someone is dead, but you can look for yourself."

His brow pinched. "No, but he's not supposed to be here, and neither are you. Who *did* find the body?"

"Come and talk to the staff." Estelle led him to the group clustered outside the building and then motioned for me to follow her. I did so, while the trolls worked on driving back the rest of the crowd of onlookers.

When Edwin moved to talk to the staff, I beckoned my cousin aside. "Professor Colt and Professor Quinn aren't outside. Do you think they're still in the other building?"

"Professor Quinn might be." Her gaze travelled over the groups of huddling students. "She's no vampire, though, and neither is the professor. This isn't their doing."

"Whose, though?" I watched as one of the trolls shouldered open the door to the labs ahead of Edwin. "Are we allowed in?"

"I'd say yes." Estelle waited for Edwin to enter and then slipped into the corridor behind him while I tailed her.

The door to the lab lay ajar, Dr Hayes's body sprawled half in the hallway. I didn't blame whoever had found her for assuming she was dead, given the gaping-mouthed look of pure terror etched on her face.

"Don't touch anything," Edwin ordered us. "You shouldn't be in here. This is a crime scene."

"Would you know she wasn't dead if we hadn't told you?" Estelle pointed at Dr Hayes's neck. "See that? Bite marks."

I moved closer, peering at Dr Hayes's pale neck. I wouldn't have spotted the bite marks if I hadn't known to look for them, but there they were—clear as daylight. Then another thought hit me. "Who's going to tell Evangeline?"

"That's a good point." Estelle looked at Edwin. He scowled in annoyance, but even he wouldn't be able to deny that if he didn't give the body over to Evangeline, she'd swoop in and probably terrorise everyone on campus in the process.

Xavier appeared through the wall so suddenly that Edwin jostled the table, causing several bottles to shake and almost topple to the floor. "This is a crime scene!"

"Sorry," Xavier said. "I—thought you ought to know there's someone hiding in the back room."

"What back room?" Edwin recovered, catching the table for balance.

"Behind the shelves." Xavier pointed at the mass of potion-laden cabinets and towering shelves at the back, which were clustered closely enough together that it wasn't surprising that we'd missed the door hidden among them. Being an elf, Edwin easily walked through the shelves without knocking into anything, but I had to tuck in my elbows and move carefully to avoid breaking any of the fragile-looking bottles when I followed.

The door, which looked like it'd been out of use for a while, was painted a faded blue and covered in cobwebs. Edwin pushed on the handle, and the door swung inward, revealing… Jesse Rogan.

"What exactly are you doing in here?" Edwin demanded.

Jesse gaped at the policeman and then seemed to shake off the initial shock. "Studying."

"You're not a student," I said for Edwin's benefit. "You were expelled."

"You." Estelle had gone chalk-white. "What did you do? Did you attack Dr Hayes?"

"He's not a vampire, Estelle," I reminded her, though the guy looked about as innocent as a masked man at a bank robbery. "Tell the police why you're here."

Jesse shuffled his feet. "I came in here to study. Then I saw Dr Hayes coming and hid in the back so she wouldn't throw me out."

"Did you see or hear who attacked her?" Edwin asked.

"No," said Jesse. "Well, I heard movement, but there's no window in here. I assumed she was tidying up."

"I see." Edwin's jaw twitched. "Come with me. You're going to answer some more questions at the police station."

"That's not fair," he protested. "I didn't do anything."

"I'll be the judge of that." Edwin gave Estelle a brief glance. "I'll contact Evangeline and ask her to take care of the body. In the meantime, I suggest the rest of you leave."

While the trolls carted Jesse off to be questioned, the rest of us were unceremoniously dismissed.

"Evangeline's going to be furious," I remarked to Estelle and Xavier as we left campus. "Lucky that Laney doesn't have a lesson tonight."

"Definitely," Xavier said. "A vampire sneaking around campus under Evangeline's nose seems like an oversight on her part."

"She did have suspicions," I said. "That was why she came to the library earlier. Though she was trying to blame Professor Colt instead."

I was even more curious about what Professor Colt would have to say for himself at tomorrow's meeting, assuming he didn't flee the town outright once he heard of the attack. He might not know about it yet, but that wouldn't last long, given the rate at which rumours spread through the small town.

"Does Evangeline think he brought the vampire with him?" Estelle asked.

"Not intentionally, if so," I said. "I mean, it's possible one of the Founders followed Professor Colt here—but why target the campus and not the library? We're at the top of their list of targets. Not Dr Hayes."

"It might not be them," Xavier said. "Professor Booker's death didn't look like their handiwork."

I shook my head. "That Jesse ticks all the boxes for the obvious culprit for both incidents—except for having fangs. What was he even doing in that room?"

"I hope Edwin will get some answers from him," said Xavier. "He might be a loose cannon, but he's in police custody now, and he'll know he can't bluff his way out of this one."

"I can't believe he managed to sneak back on campus in the first place," Estelle said. "Much less into the lab... but I can't see him being responsible for this attack. Unless he's made friends with the vampires, but why would he target Dr Hayes?"

"Because she was a witness?" I suggested. "To Professor Booker's death."

"Jesse was the one who told her about his death to begin with." Estelle's brow pinched. "How is this getting *more* complicated?"

"Good question." We reached the library and entered. "Sleep on it. Some ideas might come to you when you aren't expecting them."

While Estelle went to get an early night, Xavier and I stayed downstairs to wait for Laney to come back. I normally liked the way the library looked in the evening, lights hovering above the lobby and casting a warm glow over the shelves. Following the attack, however, the darkness took on a more sinister cast, and I kept scanning the shadows while Xavier and I waited in the Reading Corner.

"She'll be fine, Rory," he said, running a hand through my hair. "You should go to bed."

"I'm too wound up to sleep. Not before Laney's back." The warmth of his body next to mine soothed my nerves a little. Before I met him, I'd never have thought a Reaper could be a source of warmth and comfort rather than cold darkness. "If there's a hostile vampire in town, biting people, I don't want her getting blamed."

"Evangeline will warn her," Xavier said. "I don't envy anyone who runs into the vampires' leader tonight, though."

"Nor me." I snuggled up to him. "Do you think this is a rogue vampire's doing? I don't even know what to think anymore."

"It's mostly Edwin's problem now."

"Is it?" I peered at his face in the dark. "Has anything ever *not* ended up being our problem?"

The lamplight caught the corner of his mouth as he smiled. "No… but it's nice to dream a little."

"True." I kissed him lightly. "It's not been a great day, but I can think of worse ways to end the night."

9

I'd intended to stay up until Laney returned, but my exhaustion eventually got the better of me. The following morning, I woke up with a Xavier-shaped dent beside me in the bed and a message saying that he'd had to leave a couple of hours earlier because his boss had called and ordered him to come home at once.

Oh boy. Had the Grim Reaper found out about the vampire attack? It had only been a matter of time before he did, but the Reapers and the vampires got on about as well as manticores did with everyone except Cass. Generally, the Reapers held the opinion that the vampires were cheating the laws of death, which they effectively were, but that didn't mean I envied Xavier for having to deal with both.

I replied to his message, asking him to let me know how it went with his boss, and then left my room to check if Laney had come back. I crossed the corridor with some trepidation; if she'd left town last night, she might not have even known about the attack unless Evangeline had decided to ambush her on the way back.

One way to find out. I knocked on the door a couple of

times before I heard Laney stir on the other side. "Whaaa?" she asked, her voice slurred.

"Hey—everything okay?" I called to her.

"No, someone just woke me up." She groaned. "I hope it's urgent."

"Did you hear?" I pushed the door inward. "Someone got attacked by a vampire on campus last night."

She sat bolt upright in bed. "No. I sure didn't hear *that.* Who?"

"Dr Hayes," I said. "She was bitten in the same lab where Professor Booker died. Someone called the police, thinking she was dead, but Xavier's Reaper senses didn't pick up on anything, so he went to find out the truth."

"Whoa." She fell back onto the pillow. "That's messed up. Have they caught the vampire yet?"

"No, which is why I wondered if Evangeline had told you," I said. "She might not be in a good mood tonight. Fair warning."

"Like every day ending in *y*." She yawned. "Dr Hayes... which one was that?"

"A grumpy alchemist," I replied. "She won't be thrilled to wake up as one of the undead, I'm betting."

"Who is?" Her eyes closed. "Thanks for telling me. I'll tread carefully around Evangeline later."

"Good." I backed out of the doorway. "See you later."

A snore indicated she'd already fallen back asleep. After closing the door to her room, I went back to my own, where I showered and got dressed.

I descended the stairs to find a bleary-eyed Estelle eating cornflakes in the kitchen while Sylvester perched on the table next to her and stole pieces of cereal when she wasn't looking. Someone—probably Aunt Adelaide—had also left out a plate of toast and a pot of coffee.

"Hey." I pulled out a chair and joined Estelle. "Have you

heard from campus yet?"

"Yeah." Estelle yawned. "The police were there until late questioning people, but they didn't find the vampire, whoever it was. No surprise given how fast they move."

"Laney had no idea, so at least she managed to avoid Evangeline's wrath last night." I poured cereal into a bowl. "For now."

"I think we should leave her to it." Estelle gave a faint shudder. "You know what Evangeline is like. She won't want anyone else interfering."

"If there's a rogue vampire in town, don't you think—Sylvester, stop that," I reprimanded as he stole a piece of cereal right out of my bowl. "What do *you* think of all this, anyway?"

"Me?" said the owl. "I care nothing for human nonsense."

"Technically, it's vampires, not humans," I said. "And if there's a rogue vampire in town—one of the Founders, even—it's a possible threat to the library. Including you."

Sylvester ruffled his feathers. "I fail to see what threat a vampire would pose towards the likes of me."

"What about the rest of us?" Estelle asked.

"You can't be that worried when you have two of them under the same roof as you," Sylvester said snottily.

"Two? Oh, you mean the vampire in the basement." I often forgot he was there; the vampire had been present in the library since before Grandma's death, and nobody knew who he was or how long he'd been sleeping in a coffin below our feet. "You know perfectly well that it's not those vampires I'm worried about, Sylvester. What're we supposed to do if the attackers turn out to be linked to the Founders?"

"I haven't the faintest idea, you tablespoon," said Sylvester.

"Well, I'd appreciate it if you'd help out in the library

while we figure this one out," I told him. "We've hardly seen you all week."

"Such ingratitude." The owl huffed. "I've been working tirelessly for the safety and security of the library."

He stole a last piece of cereal and swooped off out of the room, clipping me on the chin with his wing in the process.

"Did he just make that up, or has he actually been making an effort to protect us?" I asked Estelle.

"No clue." She blinked. "Where'd Xavier go? Wasn't he with you?"

"He said his boss called him." I dropped my gaze to my bowl. "I bet the Grim Reaper's not pleased by the vampire attack."

"Evangeline isn't happy, either, I bet." She yawned. "I'd say we avoid both of them and stay in the library until our meeting with the professor today."

"Right, at noon," I recalled. "I'd like to talk to Edwin as well, but I don't know that he'll be any more accommodating than he was last night. And he definitely won't be impressed if he finds out we were on campus at the time of the attack, sneaking around places we weren't supposed to be in."

"I know, but Professor Quinn was too," she said. "And—Professor Colt. If either of them is involved… the police need to know."

"They do," I agreed. "You don't think the Founders followed Professor Colt? I know he was trying not to draw their attention, but a vampire attack right after he returned to town seems suspect."

"I know," said Estelle. "And Evangeline implied she was expecting something like this too. I just don't know how it all fits together."

"If we're confused, imagine how poor Edwin must feel."

Unfortunately, the person to talk to was Evangeline, not Edwin, but she'd be asleep at this hour and would be none too happy if we showed up on her doorstep asking questions. Besides, I didn't want Estelle to come with me when I did speak to the vampires. I wouldn't expose her to risk in that way.

"Maybe we should check up on him," Estelle said. "See if Jesse's given any useful information. I'm guessing he spent the night in a cell, but I wonder if he's told the truth about why he was hiding in the lab yet."

"Or if he heard anything through the door." He might know more about the professor's death than the rest of us did, whether he'd been involved or not. "If we leave early, we should avoid running into any grumpy undead."

Once we'd finished breakfast, Estelle and I went to tell Aunt Adelaide where we were going and received the usual warning to tread carefully. Aunt Adelaide also urged us not to tell the police that we'd been on campus at the time of the attack.

"We never did tell him that Evangeline paid us a visit," I said to Estelle as we walked out into yet another dreary morning. The cold breeze off the coast blasted drizzle into our faces, and I huddled in my cloak for warmth. "That might make him more inclined to connect the two incidents without us needing to mention we were sneaking around campus."

"That's true," she said. "Granted, he might decide the whole thing should be up to the vampires to investigate, but that's better than denying the professor's death was anything but an accident."

"Exactly." I ducked my head against another gust of wind as we crossed the square and followed the narrow street to the seafront.

Edwin wasn't in the police station lobby, but one of his troll guards stood near the doors at the back corner that led to the interrogation rooms and holding cells. The troll gave us both a cheery wave when we entered and then wrinkled his brow. "What're you doing here?"

"We have more information about the incident at the university campus last night," Estelle answered. "I think Edwin's going to want to know this."

"I'm going to want to know what?" Edwin walked out of the interrogation room and surveyed the pair of us. "Information, you say?"

I drew in a breath. "Evangeline paid a visit to the library yesterday afternoon, a few hours before the attack on Dr Hayes. She heavily implied the Founders were involved in Professor Booker's death, and now that someone's been attacked by a vampire, I'm inclined to think she might have been right."

Edwin's jaw twitched. "Why exactly would she tell *you* rather than reporting her suspicions to the police?"

"You really need to ask that question? This is Evangeline we're talking about." I shook my head. "How cooperative was she yesterday after you reported the attack on Dr Hayes? I mean, did you talk to her?"

"No..." He cleared his throat. "She picked up Dr Hayes and left campus without asking for my opinion."

"Not very cooperative, then," Estelle concluded. "Also, we ran into an old friend up on the campus. Professor Colt. Remember him?"

I glanced at Estelle in surprise; I'd assumed she'd want to wait until after our meeting before mentioning his name to the police.

"Who?" Edwin's expression showed no signs of recognition.

"He was the one my dad gave a book to..." I was never sure how much Edwin knew about my entanglements with the Founders, and I didn't want to place him in unnecessary danger by telling him more than he needed to know. "Professor Colt thought he was in danger from the Founders, so he left town. Now he turns up again, and two people are dead. Well, one's *un*dead."

"You're accusing this man of murder?" he asked.

"No, but someone may have followed him here," I corrected. "Evangeline was the one who tipped me off about him being back in town when she showed up at the library, and she heavily implied the Founders were involved. I don't think we should discount a warning from the vampires' leader, do you?"

Edwin took in a measured breath. "I wasn't aware the vampires took any interest in the university."

"Neither was I until she told me," I said. "Have you opened an investigation into Professor Booker's death yet?"

"No, I haven't," he said wearily. "I haven't yet received the full results of the autopsy, and besides, the attack on Dr Hayes yesterday has only complicated matters further. Plainly, Professor Booker was not attacked by a vampire."

"Even if he wasn't, he died in the same spot where Dr Hayes was attacked," said Estelle.

"I'm aware." Edwin exhaled in a sigh. "Evangeline did say that she'd find the person responsible for the attack, and frankly, I'd rather leave her to it, wouldn't you?"

"I would, but she's already tried to make it our problem," I pointed out. "And she has Laney spending nights looking for the Founders' hiding places too."

"I fail to see what you think I can possibly do about that," he said. "I have no authority over what happens on the campus, either, despite what certain students' parents seem to believe."

"What—Nova's family?" Estelle paused. "I heard that Nova got expelled for blowing up a lab… and both Nova and Jesse were expelled by Professor Booker. On that note, is Jesse in here somewhere?"

"Not for long." He gestured to the troll outside the door to the holding cells. "Now we're here, you might as well bring him out."

I stared at Edwin. "You're letting him go?"

"He's going to receive a fine for being on campus when he wasn't supposed to be, but otherwise, nothing connects him to the attack on Dr Hayes," said Edwin.

"But—" I broke off when the door at the back swung open and the troll emerged, dragging Jesse along with him. Jesse looked somewhat dishevelled after a night in jail, and he glared across the room at Edwin. "Let me go! I'm innocent!"

What's he playing at? Even if Jesse *was* innocent, which I very much doubted, he'd been hiding in the back room during the vampire attack.

"Edwin," I said in a low voice, "did he mention hearing anything from the back room when Dr Hayes was attacked? Anything he didn't mention earlier?"

"No, he didn't," Edwin said distractedly. "Jesse, you're free to go, provided you stay away from the campus."

When the troll released him, Jesse sprang towards the door like a mouse released from a trap. Estelle hastened to follow him through the automatic doors. "Jesse—excuse me, can I ask you a question?" she asked.

"No," he said shortly. "I've had enough of that from the police. What do you two want with me?"

"You were in the lab when Dr Hayes was attacked." I joined them outside, hearing Edwin's exasperated sigh as the doors closed behind me. "Were you there when Professor Booker was killed as well? You must have been if you found his body."

"I told you I had nothing to do with that," he growled. "And I'm not a vampire either. See? No fangs." He bared his teeth in demonstration.

"I can see that," Estelle said, "but you *did* find the body.

Were you by any chance hiding in the back room then as well?"

"I told you I couldn't see anything through that door, didn't I?"

"Why're you so interested in the lab?" Estelle pressed.

"I can take an academic interest, you know."

"Not if you were expelled." Estelle pursued him down the walkway. "What were you doing in the lab, exactly?"

"If you must know, I was fixing my spell," he said over his shoulder. "My Spell Assistant. The translation feature was malfunctioning."

"Translation feature, you say?" Aunt Candace popped up from behind a lamppost, startling all of us—including Jesse.

"What… did you follow us?" Had she been lurking out of sight near the police station the whole time?

"I'm shocked and insulted that you'd think such a thing of me, Rory." Aunt Candace was focused on Jesse, though, and her expression turned eager. "Did you say you had a translation spell?"

"Yes," he said. "I left it back in the labs, so I'm going to get it back."

"You're not going back to campus," Estelle said flatly. "Didn't you just get fined for trespassing?"

"I'll get the spell," Aunt Candace announced. "I was going that way myself."

She has got to be kidding me. "No, you weren't."

"Are you interested in using the Spell Assistant?" Jesse asked Aunt Candace. "It'll cost you, but there's nothing the spell can't do."

"Can it crack an unreadable code?" Aunt Candace enquired.

"I don't see why not."

"Aunt Candace!" Estelle said in a tone so sharp that it might have belonged to a different person. "We are *not* bringing this man into our family's business. As for the spell, if it's in the labs, it's evidence, and it should be handed to the police."

"The police let me go!" Jesse protested.

"Whatever the case, you aren't allowed on campus," she said. "I'll go there myself. Aunt Candace, *you* can go back to the library and tell my mother exactly why you think it's worth asking for help from a murder suspect and a criminal."

She stepped around Jesse and power-walked past the clock tower towards the square. I hurried to catch up to her, suspecting that my aunt wouldn't be cowed by her outburst in the least. Sure enough, while Estelle and I crossed the square, Jesse and Aunt Candace were in close pursuit. Despite the furious looks Estelle levelled over her shoulder, Aunt Candace continued to ask Jesse questions about his translation spell. Although I would have gone into the library for backup, Estelle was forging ahead like a rampaging manticore, and I didn't dare take my eyes off her in case she cracked and turned Aunt Candace and Jesse into pigeons or something.

After possibly the most awkward and tense few minutes of my life, we reached the campus gates. Then Estelle turned to Jesse. "Did you hear nothing I told you? You can't come in."

"I wasn't going inside." His jaw set. "I want my spell back."

"I'm not making any promises." Estelle ignored Aunt Candace altogether and marched ahead of me onto campus.

Aunt Candace chuckled behind me. "She gets more like her mother every day."

"You're unbelievable." I walked behind Estelle, hoping that Aunt Candace and Jesse both stayed put, and was relieved to spot a security guard standing nearby. Talking to…

Wait. What was Evangeline doing here?

10

I came to a halt, completely unprepared to see Evangeline on the university campus during the day and talking to a shell-shocked-looking security guard. I glanced behind me and spied Jesse ducking out of sight from the gates. At least he'd think twice about sneaking onto campus with the head of the vampires around.

"Ah, Aurora." Evangeline left the guard rooted to the spot and glided towards Estelle and me. "I wondered if I'd see you here."

"You… did?" I asked uncertainly. "Erm, is Dr Hayes in the church? The new vampire, I mean?"

"Yes, she is." Her fangs showed, revealing her discontent. "Until she wakes and can describe her attacker, however, we must look elsewhere for the source."

"So… you don't know who bit her either." I'd expected not, but I had to wonder how a strange vampire had slipped Evangeline's notice. "Do you think it's connected to Professor Booker's death too?"

"I believe the police ought to take care of that investigation themselves."

Yeah, but we both know it'll take more proof. I didn't want to mention the Founders while in potential hearing distance of strangers—not to mention Jesse and Aunt Candace, the latter of whom stood with her ears pricked as if mining our words for book ideas.

"Edwin wasn't convinced when I spoke to him," I said. "He's reluctant to accept that Professor Booker's death wasn't an accident, and he said you wanted to look for the vampire yourself..."

"Yes, which includes questioning possible witnesses." She swivelled towards the gates, where Jesse had tried to edge out of sight, and then glided in that direction. "I wonder if this individual saw the vampire responsible?"

Jesse stumbled over his own feet in an attempt to retreat from her, his bravado evaporating like water in a desert. "I didn't see anyone. I swear."

"Really," Evangeline said. "I don't think you're being truthful."

Had she read his mind? If she had, she'd have seen straight through all his excuses.

"I didn't!" he said, panicking. "I'm innocent, I promise."

He turned tail and ran as if he had a dragon on his tail. I expected Evangeline to chase him, but she didn't. She remained beside the gates with the corners of her mouth turned up in amusement. Or anger. It was kind of hard to tell. Aunt Candace glowered at me, as if it was my fault Jesse had come to campus when a wrathful vampire was present, but even she didn't dare start an argument with Evangeline.

I raised a brow. "Well, that was illuminating. What did you read from Jesse's thoughts?"

"Oh, I didn't read anything from his thoughts," Evangeline said. "I just thought you could use some help getting rid of him."

"Erm... thanks?"

"You're welcome." She gave me a fanged smile and walked through the gates. "I must return home, but do tell me if you find out anything interesting, Aurora, won't you?"

Aunt Candace stepped out of Evangeline's path so swiftly she might have been a vampire herself, while Estelle and I watched in bafflement.

"What was that about?" Estelle asked. "Weird."

"Just when I thought she couldn't surprise me any more than she already has." I shook my head. "I guess she didn't want to stop and chat."

"No... does she know we're meeting Professor Colt later?"

"She might." If she'd peered into our thoughts, she would certainly be aware, but she might also have guessed that we'd set up a meeting after she'd tipped us off that he was in town. Who knew. "What was she asking security about, do you know?"

"I'll ask." She walked up to the burly man Evangeline had been talking to, who'd remained rooted to the spot with a glazed look in his eyes. I didn't really blame him. Evangeline was a lot, even when you'd met her as frequently as I had.

The man blinked a couple of times and then noticed our approach. "Can I help you with something?"

"You were talking to Evangeline," Estelle said. "Was she here to ask about the attack?"

"Ah... yes." Some clarity came back to his expression. "Yes, she informed me of her intent to send her people to patrol campus to look for further intrusions. I was glad to accept her help."

He sounded more resigned than glad, though nobody in their right mind would turn down an offer for protection from the vampires' leader.

"Have you seen Jesse Rogan recently?" asked Estelle. "I

don't know if you heard he was fined by the police for being on campus last night..."

"Him?" The guard shook his head. "I haven't seen him since the police escorted him out."

"Didn't you see him over there?" Estelle pointed at the gates. "He wants to get his... erm, Spell Assistant. Whatever it's called. Did you confiscate anything from the labs after the police left?"

He shook his head again. "Evangeline told none of us to touch anything in there."

"Since when did you take orders from the vampires?" Estelle pursed her lips in annoyance. "Never mind. Thanks for talking to us."

As we left the confused man behind, I fell into step with her. "Did Evangeline dazzle him a little?"

"More than a little," she said. "She must have wanted to ensure he didn't turn down her offer of help, but I doubt anyone would have. Even Edwin."

"She has her people patrolling campus." That should have been a reassuring thought, but it was coupled with the notion that the Founders had got into town right under Evangeline's nose. "That means she expects another attack."

"Why, though?" Estelle wove between the buildings towards the alchemy department and the labs. "That's what I don't understand. Why would they target campus and not the library? We have far more reason to draw their attention."

"True, but we also have defences that most places don't have." Shivers sprang to my arms all the same. I knew that the people who'd be happy to see my entire family dead had set foot here when Estelle and I been on campus ourselves. "I don't know their reasoning, but I doubt Evangeline would start a panic for no reason."

"Weird that she sealed off the crime scene." Estelle's steps slowed when she reached the right building. The door was cordoned off with police tape, but otherwise, it didn't look any different than it had the previous night. "Where's Xavier when you need him?"

"I should have asked him to come with us." Not many people were around, but if we moved the police tape, I could almost guarantee someone would notice. "I wonder if Professor Quinn is still around?"

"Might be," she said. "I expect she'll know about the attack, though I have a hard time imagining she was involved."

"Unless she's secretly a vampire." No... I had a hard time seeing her attacking Dr Hayes. "While we're here, it might be worth asking her if there's anything she forgot to tell us yesterday."

"True." She eyed the cordoned-off door, her shoulders slumping. "Assuming Evangeline hasn't scared her off."

I doubted Professor Quinn had run into the head vampire, though last night's incident might have frightened her away from campus regardless. We wouldn't know until we looked, so we made for the theory department.

Estelle sought out Professor Quinn's office and knocked on the door. To my surprise, the professor answered right away. She looked as if she hadn't slept a wink the previous night, her eyes bloodshot and her hair dishevelled. "Did you hear—?"

"Dr Hayes was bitten by a vampire—I know," Estelle said. "Were you still on campus at the time?"

"No," she said. "I went home shortly after you left and then got the call later that evening telling me there'd been an attack. They haven't caught the vampire yet, I heard."

"You heard right," Estelle said. "The question is, why would a vampire trespass into the lab where Professor Booker died?"

"I told you I didn't have anything to do with that." Professor Quinn's voice wavered. "You can't possibly want to accuse me of attacking Dr Hayes too. I'm no friend of the vampires."

"No, but you knew Professor Booker, and *he* was involved with the vampires in some way, wasn't he?" I pressed. "Also, he and Dr Hayes were attacked in the same spot. Even if it wasn't the same killer, I find it hard to believe that's a coincidence, given how few people use that lab."

The colour seeped out of her face with each word I spoke. "I don't know anything about the attack, but that Jesse Rogan was arrested yesterday, wasn't he?"

"The police let him go earlier today," Estelle told her. "Also, his spell is still in the lab, I think. You know, his portable plagiarism device."

"Portable plagiarism device?" she echoed. "I've never heard of such a thing."

"He called it a Spell Assistant, and he was carting it around in a briefcase," Estelle explained. "I gather he used that to generate the essay that got him expelled. Anyway, did you have time to ask your colleagues about Jesse's recent behaviour?"

"Only that he was widely disliked and known to have made threats towards the staff when he was caught cheating," she replied. "Yet—the police let him go?"

"They did," I said, "but they still aren't investigating Professor's Booker's death as a murder. I know you don't want to draw attention to your affair, but you have a legitimate reason to call them if you've heard reports from the other staff of Jesse making threats."

"I suppose I do." She looked between us, her shoulders hunched. "As for that Professor Colt... have you spoken to *him* about this?"

"We're meeting him later," I replied. "I'm almost certain

he does have insights to offer, but I have a hard time believing Professor Booker told you nothing that might have indicated why someone would want him dead. Or why the vampires would take an interest in the university."

"No… he did." She spoke quietly, as if the words pained her. "He mentioned some of his ideas, but I didn't know he took them *seriously…* He was a professor of theory, not an alchemist."

"What ideas?" Estelle asked. "Tell us."

She dropped her gaze. "You might know that he had something of an interest in rare manuscripts, and he recently mentioned one that made reference to a potion with a unique effect… a poison so potent that it could stop even the undead heart of a vampire."

A poison that works on vampires. My own heartbeat quickened. If the Founders had got wind that such a poison existed, it wasn't hard to imagine the potential consequences. "What—was that why he was in the lab?"

"No—not at all," she said. "He was no alchemist, like I said. But he was interested in the manuscripts, and he wanted to find out if there was any truth to the rumour."

"How many people knew about this?" If word had made it to the Founders, someone must have been responsible. "Aside from you?"

"Professor Colt will have known," said Professor Quinn. "Other than that, I didn't think he took it seriously enough to draw… untoward attention."

Hmm. Had Dr Hayes known, then? She'd been in the labs at the time, but she was in a coma and unable to answer any questions herself for now. As for Professor Colt, if he'd heard about the vampire attack, he might have left the country altogether this time around.

"Someone must have found out." Estelle's voice was hushed, shocked. "Professor Quinn—did you know the vampires' leader was on campus a minute ago? She wants answers, too, and if you're hiding anything, you're better off sharing it with us than having Evangeline pluck it from your thoughts without your permission."

Professor Quinn swallowed. "I'm telling the truth. There's nothing more I know, and the vampires would have no reason to come after me."

"I hope you're right," I said. "Is Professor Colt still around?"

"I haven't a clue," she said, "but I'm keeping an eye out in case he tries to get into Charles's office again. Before you ask, I don't know what he's looking for."

"Knowledge of how to poison vampires, probably," Estelle said in a strained tone. "I never would have thought… How could he?"

"Come on." I took her arm, sensing she was either about to break out in hysterical laughter or burst into tears. "Let's get some air."

It was raining again, and the damp air seemed to soak up some of Estelle's shock. After a few moments, she came to her senses. "Well… what's done is done. Whatever the professor was up to, he's not around to tell us the truth."

"I bet Professor Colt knows," I said, "but he doesn't want to draw the vampires' attention. Given what happened to Dr Hayes, I don't blame him either."

"Poison." Estelle lowered her head. "Professor Booker died by poisoning. Is it a stretch to wonder if it was the same poison he was researching?"

"What—the poison that's deadly to vampires?" I lowered my voice, though few people were wandering around in the rain. "He wasn't trying to *make* the poison, surely. Research alone would have been enough for the Founders to take an interest."

"If all he wanted to do was research, he could have stayed in his own office," Estelle said. "Why go into the labs?"

"I… don't know." She knew the professor better than I did, but why make a poison when one didn't intend to use it? "Where's this manuscript, then? Was it in his office?"

"Not that I saw." Indecision etched itself on Estelle's face, and she swivelled back to the theory building. "I looked in the obvious places, and it's possible the manuscript wasn't written in English anyway."

"Or he left it in the lab…" I cut off that thought; we needed Xavier's help before doing any more snooping. "Wait. I wonder if Nova knew? She was in the lab, and she's not in a vampire-induced coma."

"True," she said doubtfully. "I guess it's worth dropping in and talking to her again. Then we need to find Professor Colt before he does a runner. Pity I never found out his address."

"If he's left town, Xavier can find him using his Reaper powers," I said. "But Nova won't be on campus for much longer, either, and she's the only other possible witness."

"We'll talk to her, then," she decided. "Then I'll decide what to do about that Spell Assistant thing."

"Good call," I said. "I wouldn't be surprised if Jesse tried to come back here later, after he was sure Evangeline was gone."

"And Aunt Candace." She veered towards the campus accommodation. "She's crossing a line if she thinks it's okay to ask a possible criminal to help her."

"Yeah, that was weird even for her," I commented. "I don't want her sharing the code in my dad's journal with him either."

"Definitely not," she said. "Right—let's see what Nova has to say about last night."

11

We entered the building where Nova lived and climbed past the inflatable manticore on the way upstairs. My thoughts churned with possibilities. *Did the professor expel Nova because she found out what he was doing and he didn't want her telling tales?* Or was my mind making connections that didn't exist?

Estelle found the right door and knocked. Several thumps answered, interspersed with cursing, before Nova's head poked out of the gap in the doorframe. "You again? I thought I had until the end of the week to leave campus. I'm waiting for my parents to show up and help me get this stuff out."

"Did you hear what happened last night?" asked Estelle. "The vampire attack?"

"Vampire attack?" She pushed the door open a little farther, revealing messy piles of boxes and suitcases. "No. Wait—you mean here, on campus?"

"Dr Hayes was attacked in the lab," I said. "You must have seen the commotion outside yesterday evening. She was bitten by a vampire."

"I saw the police, but I didn't know it was a *vampire*." Her eyes grew round. "You're serious? A vampire? Here?"

"The weird part," Estelle said, "was that Dr Hayes was attacked in the same lab where Professor Booker was found dead. The one you blew up."

"What?" Comprehension dawned on Nova. "You can't think I had anything to do with that, surely."

"We're not saying you had anything to do with the attack," I said, "but you spent a lot of time in the lab, didn't you? Did you hear Professor Booker or Dr Hayes say anything that might have drawn, ah, unwanted attention from the vampires?"

"Why would a vampire want anything with us?" Despite her insistent tone, she didn't quite meet my eyes and held onto the door with the air of someone looking for an excuse to close it in our faces.

"Nova," Estelle said in a gentle tone, "you can be honest with us. If you're leaving campus soon, it doesn't matter if you tell us what you heard, does it?"

"I don't have anything to tell you." The confidence had faded from her voice. "I don't know anything about the vampires. You're asking the wrong person."

"Have you heard of the Founders?" I asked, braced for a reaction.

Nova shuffled back over the threshold, tripped over a box, and landed in a sprawling heap. "Ow."

"You know the name." Estelle caught the door in one hand before it could close on us. "The Founders."

Nova lifted her head. "Please don't tell them. It was a mistake. I didn't mean to overhear."

"Overhear what?" I pressed. "Professor Booker was investigating something that caught their attention, right? We already had that confirmed by at least one person who knew him, so it doesn't matter if you tell us more."

She scrambled upright. "No. Yes. They can read my mind. I don't have one of those amulet thingies... I mean, ignore what I just said."

Aha. "Someone on campus has one of those pendants?" I asked. "The mind-reading-proof ones?"

"There's a mind-reading-proof pendant?" she asked, unconvincingly.

"Yes," Estelle said. "We've encountered them before. And so have you, I'm guessing."

"No." Nova ducked her head as if she wanted the pile of boxes to swallow her up. "I don't have one. If I knew what they were. Which I don't."

"Well, we do," I told her. "And we know they come from the Founders. Are they recruiting from among the students?"

She shook her head violently. "No. Not that I've heard of. I've never seen them—it's true."

That doesn't mean they haven't been here. Nova wasn't an obvious target, since she spent most of her time in the lab rather than intentionally causing trouble like, say, Jesse Rogan.

"What about Jesse?" I asked. "He was hanging out in the lab, wasn't he?"

Her shoulders tensed. "Yeah, but he wouldn't talk to me, so I let him get on with it."

"Get on with what?"

She shrugged. "I don't know. Whatever experiment he was doing. Why does it matter?"

"It matters because the Founders tend to inflict punishment on anyone who crosses them," Estelle said. "And two people died in that lab. Whether it was the Founders' work or not, if you heard anything that might help us..."

"I don't get why you're interested," Nova protested. "How do *you* know about the—the Founders?"

"For a start, we're living in the same library as a vampire,"

I told her. "The head of the local vampires visits me on a regular basis, and that library is on the Founders' list of targets and has been there for months. Of course, we know about them."

Nova gaped at me for a moment. "Your library's on their list?"

"Has been for months, yes," I said. "It won't change anything for us if you tell us the truth."

"You spoke to him, didn't you?" Estelle asked. "Professor Booker. Why exactly did he expel you, aside from blowing up the lab?"

"That was all there was." She lowered her head. "I didn't do anything else. It was an accident."

"You know you can't get into any more trouble than you already are, don't you?" Estelle queried. "The only other witness aside from Jesse Rogan got herself bitten by a vampire and can't talk, so we'd be grateful if you filled in some of the gaps. Preferably *before* anyone else gets hurt."

"I..." She trailed off. "I may have accidentally destroyed something Professor Booker was working on when I blew up the lab. He was making some kind of potion."

The poison? If she'd accidentally destroyed a sample of the poison that worked on vampires, it might explain why he'd been angry enough to expel her—but why would he have been trying to brew the poison himself to begin with?

"Is that all?" I asked. "The whole story?"

"Yeah." Her shoulders slumped. "He was furious. I was kind of hoping he'd change his mind when he calmed down, but he's dead now, and it's too late."

"Did he talk to you about what he was making?" asked Estelle.

"No... he mostly talked to himself," she said. "I heard some of it, though. Not on purpose. He forgot I was there."

"We're not here to judge you for being curious," said

Estelle. "Professor Booker was my mentor, and if you know anything about his death that'll stop it happening to anyone else..."

"I don't know about his death," she said, "but when he first showed up in the lab, he was working on a translation of an old recipe he found in a manuscript. He was having trouble figuring it out, so he borrowed this spell..."

"From Jesse?" Estelle guessed. "You mean the Spell Assistant?"

"That was what he called it, yes," Nova said. "I don't know where he got it, before you ask. He certainly didn't make it himself. It's way too advanced."

"Where is it now?" Estelle asked. "Still in the lab?"

"I thought Jesse took it everywhere with him." She inhaled. "Look, I really didn't have anything to do with whoever attacked Dr Hayes. Or who killed the professor. I'm just lying low until my parents can come and help me move out."

"Didn't they threaten to sue the university?" Estelle asked. "Are you sure you want to invite them to campus?"

Nova's face flushed. "They just want what's best for me."

"Well, you might want to ask them not to bother the police," I told her. "They have enough to deal with."

"I'll tell them," she said. "Is that all? I'm not being arrested?"

"Of course not," Estelle said. "I have one last question... Have you seen Professor Colt recently?"

"Him?" she asked. "No... not that I know of. I thought he left."

I'd have to take her word for it on that one. It sounded as if she'd just been in the wrong place at the wrong time, and with any luck, we'd get the rest of the story from Professor Colt, whether he was in town or not.

"He did," said Estelle. "Ah—if you like, I can put in a

request with the head of the university to reconsider your case. I think Professor Booker would have wanted me to."

"Really?" Nova leaned forward, her eyes glittering with tears. "Would you?"

"Yeah, of course. Blowing up a lab isn't an expellable offence." Estelle gave her a brief smile. "Talk later."

"What now?" I asked Estelle in a low voice as we climbed downstairs. "It's safe to say Professor Booker was closer to creating the poison than we thought. If that was what she destroyed."

"I don't know," Estelle said. "He wasn't an alchemist, and neither is Professor Colt, come to that—but he doesn't need to have succeeded for the Founders to take notice."

"No." I ducked around the inflatable manticore on the way downstairs. "I don't know about you, but I want to have another look in that lab without waiting until after dark."

"Before Jesse comes back for the briefcase," added Estelle. "What—you're going to ask Xavier to help?"

"That's the plan." If the professor had borrowed the Spell Assistant for himself, it was more valuable than it appeared.

And if Professor Colt had indeed left town, the one person who'd be able to find him was Xavier.

I fired off a message to Xavier, and since we didn't have to contend with the library's tendency to muffle my phone signal, I received a reply right away.

"Finally, some good news." I slipped my phone back into my pocket. "He's on his way."

Estelle and I went to meet Xavier near the gates. He bypassed security with ease, his Reaper stealth rivalling a vampire for unobtrusiveness. Which didn't say much for the campus security's ability to find the intruder, really.

Xavier greeted me with a brief hug. "More breaking and entering?"

"Yeah—we need to look in the lab," I explained. "Jesse left

his briefcase in there, and nobody has confiscated it yet. The door's cordoned off..."

"Not a problem," he said. "Anything you want me to look out for?"

"Erm..." During my own glimpse of the lab, I'd not had the skills to tell one bottle from another, and Xavier wasn't even a wizard. "Old manuscripts. Papers. Anything that looks like it might belong to someone trying to replicate an old recipe for a poison that works on vampires."

His eyes widened. "All right... you'll have to tell me the rest of it later. I'll be thirty seconds."

He was too. In a flash—or whatever the shadowy equivalent was—he reappeared at my side, holding Jesse's briefcase in his hand.

"You weren't kidding." Estelle shook her head in admiration. "Find any papers?"

"Nothing," he replied. "A lot of potion bottles, yes, but nothing else was in the back room, and the lab looks like it's been tidied up since the last time."

Weird. If Professor Booker had had the manuscript with him when he'd died, where'd it disappeared to?

Estelle's expression turned dark. "At least we have that so-called Spell Assistant. I'd say we should hand it over to the police."

"Would Edwin know what to do with it?" I asked sceptically. "It looks more like something the curse-breaker would take an interest in."

"It's not cursed, though." Estelle took the briefcase from Xavier's outstretched hand, and we headed for the gates. On the way, I told Xavier of our conversations with Professor Quinn and Nova, briefly. I didn't want to give too much detail in case Evangeline's vampire allies were to be listening in, but I saw no signs of anyone patrolling the gates.

When we reached the fence alongside the local cemetery,

Xavier said, "My boss wants me to report in, but I can drop by the library later. That okay?"

"Sure." I wrapped him in a hug. "Estelle and I are going to meet Professor Colt at noon. We might need your help to find him."

"Better save that for a last resort." He gave me a brief kiss and withdrew behind the cemetery's fence, which remained shrouded in darkness even during the day.

As I descended the high street, a screeching noise that sounded suspiciously like an owl reached my ears.

"Was that from the pet shop?" I caught up to Estelle, who'd halted, the briefcase swinging in her grasp. "It sounded like…"

"Sylvester?" Alarm flitted across her face.

In unison, we broke into a swift stride towards the square. *The library can't be under attack. The Founders wouldn't come here in broad daylight.*

They hadn't—but a crowd had gathered in the square in front of the library, where Sylvester had perched on the top of the door. Crouched on the steps in front of him was none other than Jesse Rogan.

"What's up with him?" Estelle jogged up alongside me. "He doesn't normally make that kind of racket outside."

"Unless…" I spied Aunt Candace hovering near the steps. "Please tell me Aunt Candace didn't invite that Jesse into the library to help her with her translation."

"She didn't, did she?" Estelle swore under her breath. "What's wrong with her?"

"Many things," I said, "but it sounds like the library's guard dog… or owl… said no thanks."

While it was gratifying to know Sylvester had been watching out for us, Aunt Candace did not look pleased. Jesse began yelling obscenities at the door as I glimpsed Aunt Adelaide peering out of the window.

"There you are." Aunt Candace spotted the pair of us and beckoned with one hand. "Can't one of you reason with that owl? My sister is refusing to listen too."

"Are you trying to bring that guy into the library?" I said in a low voice when I caught up to her. "He just got fined by the police for trespassing, you know."

"That's right," Estelle put in. "Can you see past your own interests for five minutes?"

"Hey!" Jesse noticed us—or specifically, the briefcase in Estelle's hands. "That's mine."

Estelle held her ground when he began to stalk towards us. "This was found at a crime scene, Jesse. It needs to be handed over to the police."

"Absolutely not," Aunt Candace said in scandalised tones. "I need to use it."

"You can't bring an untested and unknown spell into the library, Aunt Candace," I told her. "Have some sense."

"It's been tested plenty," Jesse growled. "Get that animal away from me."

Sylvester flew from the door and followed Jesse, his wings beating menacingly.

"Aunt Candace, do you really want to trust a guy who was hiding in the back room of a lab while a murder was being committed?" Estelle hissed. "I don't think so. Besides, we don't know where he even got this spell."

"That's because it's none of your business." Ignoring the owl, Jesse held out a hand for the briefcase. "Give it to me."

"Not until you promise to stay away from the library," Estelle said firmly. "And the campus too."

"The library's a public space," he retaliated. "I should be able to go wherever I like. And your aunt wants to hire me."

"I do," Aunt Candace said. "Really, that owl is out of hand."

Sylvester gave a hoot that made Jesse falter, while Estelle swung the briefcase out of reach.

I seized Aunt Candace's arm and whispered, "Please think for a moment. Even if that guy's not involved with the Founders, he strikes me as someone who'd sell that information to them without blinking an eye."

"You make a very good point," she said. "I shall consider—"

Sylvester interrupted by diving straight at Estelle with a screech. She took a startled step back as the owl's beak clamped over the handle of the briefcase and yanked it out of her grip. Then he flew towards the library with the briefcase dangling from his beak, ignoring the startled gasps that followed him.

"Did you see that?" Jesse spluttered. "I just got robbed by an owl. Thief!"

He screamed at the top of his lungs, but Sylvester paid no attention. The door to the library nudged open, and the owl disappeared inside, briefcase and all.

What in the hell was that?

12

I ducked into the library after Sylvester, Jesse's yells ringing in my ears. The owl flew on, above a baffled Aunt Adelaide and the even more startled patrons browsing the stacks or sitting in the Reading Corner.

"Sylvester!" I called to him. "What are you doing with that briefcase?"

I'd thought he'd deemed the spell too dangerous to bring into the library. I certainly hadn't expected him to take it for himself with his own hands—or beak, rather.

Sylvester ignored me, soaring upward until he disappeared over the third-floor balcony. Cursing, I ran for the stairs, leaving behind Jesse's indignant shouting. I hoped Aunt Adelaide and Estelle could hold him off, because Sylvester had dropped all security guard duties in favour of committing robbery. In front of a crowd. I could only imagine the resulting rumours, but I couldn't do anything except mitigate the damage by catching our rogue owl.

I ran all the way up the twisting staircase to the first floor then the second. At the third, I rested a hand on the balcony to catch my breath and glimpsed Sylvester flying towards the fourth-floor corridor's colour-changing door.

"What *are* you doing, Sylvester?" I wheezed, breaking into an exhausted jog to catch him up. "I thought you wanted to keep—that spell *out* of the library. Not steal it."

Sylvester growled around the briefcase in his beak but didn't reply until he touched down in front of the door. As he landed, a bewildered Cass stuck her head out of the door to the Magical Creatures Division. "What's with the racket?"

"Sylvester stole a dodgy translation spell," I said between breaths. "From a shady guy who may or may not be allied with the Founders."

"Really?" she said. "Good job, Sylvester."

"Seriously?" I said blankly.

The owl gave a sweeping bow, while I wondered if everyone who'd been near the fourth-floor corridor had lost their minds.

"Am I the only person who thinks it's a bad idea to bring that thing in here?" I approached the briefcase, warily. "Sylvester, what if that spell is hostile to the library?"

"Don't you think I'd know if it was, you pencil case?"

"Well…" He had a point there. "You're still taking a risk by stealing from someone who's already made threats and possibly committed murder too. Do you really want to add him to the list of people who have reason to plot revenge on the library?"

"Was he a loyal patron? I had no idea."

"Sylvester." My eye twitched. "Seriously, you can't go around committing robbery in broad daylight."

"Interesting," he said. "I thought you established that the charming individual outside was *not* the original owner of this fascinating spell."

He'd been eavesdropping on us, had he? "That doesn't make it safe to use."

I heard footsteps and turned to the stairs, where Aunt Candace came puffing into view, having presumably run all the way up from the lobby.

"Ah, excellent." She bounded over and knelt beside the briefcase. "Many thanks, Sylvester."

"What is *wrong* with you all?" I looked to Cass for backup, but she'd withdrawn back into the Magical Creatures Division and closed the door, while Aunt Adelaide and Estelle were probably still dealing with Jesse downstairs. "This spell is the property of the person who's currently my main suspect for committing murder—twice, if he had a hand in the vampire attack on Dr Hayes as well. Even if the spell wasn't his to begin with, I hardly think it's worth the risk. Aunt Candace, do you even know how to use it?"

"Not yet, but I will," she said. "Now, I'll thank you to get out from under my feet, Rory."

Her words stung, unexpectedly. I was used to my aunt's bluntness—and Sylvester's, too—but it was hardly fair of them to leave Aunt Adelaide and Estelle to deal with the consequences of their actions. I recognised a losing battle when I saw one, though.

"Fine," I said. "If you end up losing your memories or worse, don't come to me for help."

As I made for the stairs, my phone buzzed in my pocket. I fished it out as I climbed downstairs and found a message from Xavier asking if I was okay. He must have heard the ruckus and correctly guessed that it'd come from the library.

I waited until I reached the lobby before replying, where I found Estelle and Aunt Adelaide barring the door from the inside.

"Where's that spell?" Estelle asked over her shoulder. "Did Sylvester hide it?"

"He gave it to Aunt Candace." I sent a response to Xavier explaining the situation in brief, though it was impossible to sum up its entirety in a text message. "You're not closing the library, are you?"

"Until the police come and remove Jesse, it's not safe to leave the doors open," Aunt Adelaide said. "That's unfortunate for our current visitors, but I assume Sylvester didn't think the spell would be a danger to any of them."

"I have absolutely no idea what he's thinking," I admitted. "He did point out that the spell wasn't Jesse's to begin with, but I hope the police show up soon."

"I know." Estelle eyed my phone when it buzzed. "Xavier?"

"Yeah, he heard the noise—and so did everyone else in town, probably," I said. "He can walk through walls, so it doesn't matter if the door's barred."

I did feel sorry for anyone else who was browsing the library, but if we opened the door, we risked Jesse getting in and wreaking havoc in an attempt to get his spell back.

"Yeah," Estelle said. The door trembled as if someone had thrown a heavy object at it from outside, and she winced. "It'd be nice if Sylvester chased off Jesse himself."

I scowled. "Yes, it would. He and Aunt Candace are being downright infuriating. Is it possible the fourth floor has eaten some of their brain cells?"

"You never know what that owl is thinking." Aunt Adelaide pointed her wand at the door, and several bolts slid into place. "I expect he has a plan."

True, but knowing Sylvester, he wouldn't tell us until after the fact. As I opened my mouth to reply, Xavier appeared through the wall.

"Hey—Rory." He eyed the barricaded door. "Jesse is trying to break into the library… why?"

"Sylvester stole his Spell Assistant," I explained. "Well—he's arguing that it isn't stealing, since the spell wasn't Jesse's to begin with, but Jesse himself doesn't see it that way."

The door trembled yet again, the wood creaking alarmingly behind the bolts. Xavier raised an eyebrow. "Do you want me to drive him off?"

"The police are on their way, but we might need help if he manages to get in," I told him. "Sylvester is upstairs with Aunt Candace, who has decided now's the perfect time to learn how to use that dodgy spell for herself."

"What about Cass?" asked Estelle. "I assume she heard the noise too."

"Yes, but I guess it wasn't interesting enough for her to leave her animals." I rubbed my forehead. "At this point, Jesse is my prime suspect for murdering Professor Booker, so it's beyond irresponsible of anyone to bring his property into the library. Edwin had better not let him go this time."

"He shouldn't," Xavier said. "Are you still planning to meet the professor later?"

"That's the plan, right, Estelle?"

"At noon, yes." Estelle paced behind the door, her wand in her hand and her shoulders tensed. "Assuming our unwanted guest is behind bars, where he belongs."

I checked the time and saw that we had less than an hour before our planned meeting. *Come on, Edwin.* Professor Colt might be able to shed some light on the disparate clues we'd gathered, though I doubted he'd want to risk his own neck—literally—by helping us take on the Founders himself. Then again, I was starting to lose faith that certain members of my own *family* would help.

Xavier inclined his head. "I'll help Edwin escort Jesse to the police station, if it helps."

"I'd hoped Sylvester might chase him off," I said. "The last I saw, he was sitting directly in front of the door he'd been ignoring for the past few weeks, which makes no sense whatsoever."

"I don't get it either," Estelle said. "Perhaps Sylvester's

having a moment. He wants to feel useful again, and he figured stealing the spell would help."

"Weird." Xavier's brow wrinkled. "He's the embodiment of the library itself, isn't he? He might think the spell is useful to the library..."

"Even if it belongs to the enemy." Unease skittered down my spine. "I wonder where Jesse originally got it. Did he find it on eBay or something?"

"Good question." Estelle spun to the door when a thumping noise came from outside. "Is that Edwin?"

"It is." Aunt Adelaide indicated the window, and when I moved closer, I spied one of Edwin's troll guards hauling an indignant Jesse down the library's steps. Another troll stood nearby, urging the crowd to leave the square.

The rumours would have already kicked off, but at least we'd be able to reopen our doors and let our patrons leave without anyone running into a deranged former student who might or might not be a murderer.

"Good riddance." Estelle watched Jesse vanish, his yells petering out. "I don't see Edwin..."

"He might not have come in person," I said. "I can't imagine he'd be happy to learn that the reason Jesse tried to break into the library was because the family's owl decided to steal his property."

"Definitely not." Aunt Adelaide moved through the shelves to the Reading Corner, where the terrified patrons had sheltered from the noise. "I'm sorry about that. You can leave now, if you like."

It never ceased to amaze me how quickly the library could return to normal following any kind of disruption. Within minutes, Estelle and I were running around helping patrons find books as if nothing had happened. Jesse remained in the back of my mind—as did whatever my aunt and Sylvester were doing up on the third floor—but before I knew it, Estelle was tugging on my arm.

"It's almost noon," she said. "What're the odds that Professor Colt skips out on our meeting?"

"Higher than the odds of Sylvester explaining why he decided to swipe that briefcase," I commented. "If he does... Xavier, would you be able to track him?"

Xavier, who'd mostly been standing unobtrusively next to the desk since Jesse's departure, tensed at my words. "I can't say my boss will be pleased if I use my Reaper powers to track a wayward professor. He's already irked at me for spending too much time at the university."

"Professor Colt definitely knows more than he let on," I said. "I don't think he's guilty of murder, but I'm almost certain Professor Booker told him the details of what he was researching."

"A poison that can kill vampires." Xavier's expression darkened. "I can see why the Founders would want to keep that knowledge in their own hands."

"Professor Colt has been avoiding them for months," said Estelle. "There's a chance he's left town, but he came back for a reason. It's worth seeing if he shows up."

We headed for the door, and Aunt Adelaide spotted us. "You're not going to the police station again, are you?"

"No, we're meeting Professor Colt," Estelle replied. "We arranged to meet on the seafront, out in the open."

"All right." Her mouth pulled down at the corners. "If you're sure."

"We'll see you in a bit." I waved to my aunt and left the library with Xavier and Estelle.

This time, the square was mostly empty aside from a few shoppers browsing the pet store and the bakery. We attracted a few curious stares but nothing too overt. It was hardly the first time a weirdo had tried to break into the library, though that didn't usually happen in broad daylight.

"I wonder if Dr Hayes has woken up yet?" Estelle said. "I keep forgetting she's stuck in Evangeline's house. What a nightmare."

"It'll be another day or two until she re-emerges as a vampire," I replied. "I don't quite get how she ended up drawn into this. Was she helping Professor Booker to brew the poison?"

"It's more likely that she was nosing around the lab and the Founders thought she was a possible witness," Estelle said. "She didn't like Professor Booker *or* Professor Quinn, and it must have really annoyed her that they were using the lab for their romantic trysts. I don't see her offering to help him."

That made sense, but we wouldn't know the truth until Dr Hayes woke up. In the meantime, we reached the seafront as the hands on the towering clock above moved towards noon.

Professor Colt was easy to spot, a tall, thin figure hovering near the pier. He hadn't run off, which was something of a surprise, though he held the look of a mouse in a trap when he watched us approaching him.

"Professor." Estelle halted in front of him. "I was wondering if you left town."

"I should have." Professor Colt's shoulders hunched inside his thick coat. "Why'd you bring the Reaper with you? Not to take my soul?"

"Don't be absurd," Estelle said. "I don't know if you heard the noise, but Jesse tried to attack the library earlier and got himself arrested."

"Good." The professor gazed at the police station. "Edwin should never have let him walk free."

"Do you suspect him of murdering Professor Booker?" I

figured we might as well start with the most pertinent question.

"I... I'm not in a position to make accusations," he mumbled. "But I don't trust him."

"Why, because he overheard Professor Booker in the lab?" Estelle took in a breath. "I know you left out some information yesterday, possibly because Professor Quinn was there—but we know Professor Booker was translating an old recipe for poison before he died. He told you, didn't he?"

Professor Colt flinched. "This isn't the place..."

"You were the one who suggested meeting here," Estelle said. "We know what he was doing. Translating a recipe for poison—one potent enough to kill a vampire. It doesn't take a genius to know who might have found out and decided to stop him."

"No, I..." He wrung his hands. "I didn't help him. I didn't go near the lab."

"He still told you what he was doing," Estelle said. "I know it was his risk to take, but—listen, why *did* you come back?"

The professor shrugged. "It's safer here... safer than the alternatives, anyway."

"Except for the vampire who slipped onto campus last night?" I frowned. "And attacked one of your colleagues?"

"As it happens," said a silky voice, "I have a few questions I'd like to ask about that incident too."

Professor Colt stood transfixed with horror as Evangeline glided into view. What in the world was she doing here? Had she also been looking for the professor?

"I... Evangeline." He swallowed. "What incident? I didn't..."

"I think you know why I'm here, Professor," she said softly. "Dr Hayes woke up, and the first thing she said was *your* name."

"What?" His voice rose to a squeak. "I'm not the one who attacked her."

"Aren't you?" Evangeline exposed her fangs. "When I'm done with you, you'll wish the Founders had caught you instead."

The chill in her voice made me want to back away, and I wasn't even on the receiving end. But my confusion won out over fear. "What are you talking about, Evangeline?"

She remained silent, her intent stare pinning the professor like an ant under a magnifying glass.

Estelle made a choked noise. "Professor Colt, what did you do?"

"I..." He squeezed his eyes shut. "Dr Hayes saw Professor Booker and me discussing the manuscript and the translation. I thought she might expose us, so I..."

"You did what?" I pressed.

"I spiked her drink with a memory potion," he mumbled. "I hoped it'd make her too groggy to remember anything of our conversations."

"Then... she's not actually a vampire?" She hadn't been bitten at all? "Then who killed Professor Booker? Was that you too?"

"Not me." Misery laced his words. "It can't have been the Founders, though. They were never here."

"No." Evangeline's teeth gleamed. "They weren't."

The professor made a quiet, frightened noise. "Did—did Dr Hayes remember anything?"

"You can ask her yourself." Evangeline reached out a manicured hand. "You're coming with me."

13

Professor Colt spun around and bolted. He must have known trying to outrun a vampire was an exercise in futility, but Evangeline came to a gliding stop before she reached him. Xavier stood in her path, feet planted apart, arms folded across his chest.

My heart stuttered, and Estelle clutched my arm. *Xavier. What are you doing?*

Evangeline regarded Xavier with calm eyes. "I'd advise you to move, Reaper."

"It's not up to you to dispense justice against humans," he said evenly. "The professor didn't intend to provoke you, and if you attack him, you'll be liable to answer to the authorities."

His gaze flickered towards the police station while Evangeline drew herself upright, her voice icy cold. "He tried to manipulate me."

"I doubt that was his intention." Xavier nodded to Professor Colt. "Right?"

"Of course not," the professor gasped out. "I… I wanted to avoid word spreading about Charles's research, and I knew

Dr Hayes was suspicious. I used a potion I found in the labs to erase her memory, but I didn't know it'd cause her to fall into a coma—and it wasn't I who left those marks on her neck."

"I find that hard to believe." Evangeline's gaze raked over him, and I had little doubt that she was probing his thoughts for any hint of a lie. After a short pause, her eyes narrowed. "You should have been more careful. It's lucky that Dr Hayes survived, but the police might not be as inclined to believe you didn't intend permanent harm to her."

"I really didn't," he whispered. "I'm sorry. If I can do anything to make it up to you—"

"I'd start by not making bargains with vampires," she said. "You'll live longer."

And in one elegant step, she vanished, leaving the four of us alone on the seafront. Professor Colt swayed on the spot, as if he was going to faint, and even Xavier wore an expression of profound relief that the head of the vampires was gone.

"That was a close one." I inhaled. "Professor, you're lucky Xavier defended you. What were you thinking?"

"I... wasn't..."

"That's right. You weren't thinking." Estelle turned in the direction of the police station. "Edwin would be very interested to hear a confession from you."

"He... he knows?"

"No, but this isn't the vampires' problem any longer," I said. "And as soon as Dr Hayes recovers from the shock of waking up in a vampire's home, I bet the first thing she does is call the police. Even if she doesn't, Evangeline might change her mind and come back for you."

He made a choked noise. "I... all right. I'll turn myself in."

I half expected the professor to try to run again, but he complied without a fuss. I figured he thought he'd be safer behind bars than in Evangeline's clutches, which was true enough. Estelle and I flanked him, with Xavier walking at his back.

When we neared the station, the professor glanced at me. "I didn't put those fake bite marks on her neck. It's the truth. Someone else must have."

"Jesse?" I guessed. "Why would he do that?"

"Maybe he was trolling… no offence," Estelle added when we walked past one of Edwin's troll guards on the way into the police station.

I scanned the lobby just in case Jesse was there, but he wasn't. Edwin wasn't, either, though the troll regarded all of us with a puzzled expression on his craggy face.

The professor shifted on his feet. "I don't know what happened to Charles's notes on that manuscript. That was what I was looking for in his office, but they weren't there. If he left them in the lab…"

"Worry about explaining yourself to Edwin first." Estelle stepped forward as Edwin emerged from the interrogation room. "Good timing."

Edwin's gaze fell on Professor Colt. "You're the professor?"

"Yes, and he has a confession to make." I indicated the professor. "Turns out Dr Hayes wasn't attacked by a vampire at all."

"Really?" Edwin's brow arched. "That wasn't what Jesse just told me."

"He's in here?" The professor blanched. "Has he been arrested?"

"For trying to break into the library, yes," Edwin confirmed. "If you've a confession to make yourself, you'd better come with me."

He led the professor towards one of the interrogation

rooms. They were far too small to fit all of us in, so I hung back with Xavier.

"You need to head home?" I guessed.

"No—not as long as you're in danger," he said. "I don't think Edwin wants me to listen in on the questioning, though… and there's not much I can do here."

"Nor me." I caught Estelle's eye; she'd been about to walk into the interrogation room too. "Estelle—do you want to stay here while I head back to the library? I think one of us ought to be here to make sure Professor Colt doesn't leave out any details."

She nodded. "Yeah… I'll report back later. You should probably check what Sylvester and Aunt Candace are doing with that spell."

"That's true." The notion of leaving her alone wasn't appealing, but we'd already heard the professor's confession, and Jesse would be in the holding cells for the foreseeable future. "I'll see you later."

Xavier walked me back to the library. The exhaustion of the day had begun to catch up with me, though I knew Dr Hayes, for one, was having a worse day than I was.

"I wonder if she's left Evangeline's house yet?" I said to Xavier. "What a nightmare—waking up in a vampire's home when you aren't one of them."

Evangeline would want her gone as soon as possible, but her wrath was mostly directed at Professor Colt. I didn't even blame her, considering.

"I can't believe him," Xavier said. "Professor Colt… I guess he wanted to avoid Dr Hayes telling tales and accidentally getting someone else killed, but he must have known using a potion on her would land him in trouble."

"Why would someone else turn it into a fake vampire attack?" I queried. "That's what I don't get. Jesse was in the room, which makes him the obvious suspect, but if he was the one who killed Professor Booker, why not finish the job this time around?"

"I don't get it either," Xavier agreed. "Also—didn't Evangeline read his mind?"

"Jesse's?" I thought back to our encounter on campus. "I guess she didn't see him fake the vampire attack. That, or he was wearing one of those pendants, but you'd think she'd have noticed."

Weird. The Founders hadn't been on campus, but that didn't mean they weren't involved. A man was still dead, after all.

We entered the library, where Aunt Adelaide gave us both a strained smile from behind the front desk. "Rory. Xavier. Did you meet with the professor?"

"Yes, and Evangeline almost skewered him." I gave her a brief rundown of our conversation and the unexpected visit from the head of the vampires. "I don't know where Dr Hayes is now, but she won't stay in the vampires' church."

"I imagine they don't want her there either," Aunt Adelaide commented. "I can't believe the professor would have gone as far as to fake a vampire attack. Did he not think Evangeline would realise the truth?"

"I think he panicked," I said. "Dr Hayes worked in the labs, so it's a given that she'd have picked up on what Professor Booker was doing, and Professor Colt wanted to make sure word didn't make it back to the Founders. If so, I have to wonder if the professor expelled Nova and Jesse to stop them from telling tales too."

"Speaking of Jesse, I do hope he's in custody?" Aunt Adelaide queried.

"Yes, he is," I replied. "Edwin's talking to Professor Colt, and Estelle's there to make sure he doesn't leave anything out of his story. I didn't think Xavier and I would be able to help much, so I figured I'd come back and see if Aunt Candace had figured out that spell yet. Is she still upstairs?"

"Yes, with Sylvester," she said. "I assume he won't let her do anything too reckless, though I'd never have expected him to bring a potentially dangerous spell into the library either."

"Who even knows," I said. They'd refused to listen earlier, but maybe having Xavier with me this time would help. "I'll check up on them."

"It doesn't sound like they've blown anything up," Xavier remarked as we climbed the stairs.

"Don't jinx it," I told him. "My aunt already turned herself purple, and that was *before* she got hold of Jesse's portable plagiarism device."

"How does it work? Do you know?"

"No clue." I followed the curving staircase up to the first floor. "I don't know that a spell that seems designed to help students cheat on their assignments can help Aunt Candace solve Grandma's riddle, but she's determined."

Maybe the revelation of the faked vampire attack would be enough to distract her, but I had my doubts.

On the third floor, we found Aunt Candace sitting on a beanbag chair near the fourth-floor corridor door with a polished metal box resting on her knees. I might have mistaken the box for her own translator spell if I hadn't seen the briefcase lying open nearby. Sylvester perched atop a nearby shelf, watching my aunt tap buttons on the box's surface.

"Do you even know how to use that?" I asked her.

"I'm working it out," she said. "This spell is too sophisticated for simple minds. I doubt that fool of a student ever figured out how to use it."

"He used it to copy someone's essay without being in the room with them."

To my consternation, she laughed. "Simple minds indeed.

If one feeds a piece of writing into the box, it can certainly generate an endless stream of text in that same style… but that's the most basic of its settings."

"I'll take your word for it on that one." Next to her lay the paper that she'd scribbled the code on. I gathered that she hadn't inserted Grandma's riddle into the box yet, but what would happen when she did? "What can it do that the other spell can't?"

"It can *predict.*" She looked up, her eyes gleaming with excitement. "If I feed it my mother's absurd riddle, it'll do its best to provide an answer."

"Will the answer be written in plain English, though?" I looked up at the owl. "Sylvester, what do you think?"

The owl peered down at Xavier. "Did you bring the Reaper here for a reason?"

"He's here in case you set off the apocalypse when you open that box," I informed him. "Also, it might interest you to know that the vampire attack was a fake."

Sylvester didn't even blink. "Indeed."

"Did you know?" Was he even listening to me? He was focused on the box, on which several of the buttons flashed an ominous red. "I hope it's worth all this trouble, whatever it is."

Xavier crouched down next to the discarded briefcase. "What's this, the instruction manual?"

"There's a manual?" I scooted over to his side and saw a stack of papers had been tucked into the briefcase. Aunt Candace seemed to have overlooked them entirely. "Aunt Candace, look at this."

"Already did," she said without looking up. "Those aren't instructions."

"Then what…?" I picked up the papers, and my heart gave a jolt when I recognised the name on the top of the first page. "They're Professor Booker's notes."

Notes and a piece of yellowing paper that looked awfully like…

Xavier's mouth dropped open. "The manuscript."

The recipe for the poison. Jesse must have stolen the professor's notes and hidden them in the briefcase, not expecting to get caught by the police and forced to leave it behind. Professor Colt had assumed the manuscript had been in Professor Booker's office, but instead…

I lowered the papers and looked up into Sylvester's knowing eyes. "Was this why you brought the spell into the library? You knew Jesse stole Professor Booker's notes and the manuscript containing the recipe for the poison?"

Xavier swore softly. "That's got to be it. Jesse wanted the manuscript… so he killed the professor."

"Why would he have wanted the manuscript?" To sell to the Founders? "Sylvester, Jesse is in jail, and Professor Colt is going to end up joining him at this rate. If the Founders want this recipe, are you sure you want to keep it in the library?"

"I rather think this is the safest place to keep a dangerous text such as that one, don't you agree?" Sylvester replied.

"Just checking." I looked at Aunt Candace next, who continued to fiddle with the box. "Did you hear any of that?"

"Yes, it's safer in the library."

"You didn't hear a word of it." I scowled. "Aunt Candace, this manuscript contains a recipe for a poison that can stop even a vampire's heart. I'd have thought you'd be all over that."

She lifted her head briefly. "Has anyone ever succeeded in brewing this poison?"

"I…" That was a good question. Professor Booker's notes were scribbled all over the pages in a haphazard manner. He must have translated each piece of the manuscript as he went along, and the result was a mess I couldn't decipher. "I'll ask Aunt Adelaide."

"Good call," Xavier said. "Estelle will want to know, too, once she's back from the police station."

"Yeah... and Professor Colt." He wouldn't be seeing the light of day for a while, but he'd almost certainly seen the manuscript with his own eyes. "Aunt Candace, what do you think?"

"Do that."

Why do I bother? Sylvester didn't move when I turned away, but I was sure he'd intended for the manuscript to end up here in the library. I held it gingerly as Xavier and I went downstairs to the lobby.

I walked straight to the front desk. "Aunt Adelaide—these papers were in Jesse's briefcase. He stole them from Professor Booker."

"What's that?" she asked. I offered the papers to her, and she held out a hand and took them. "This isn't written in English..."

"It's the original recipe for a poison that can kill vampires," I said in an undertone. "And Professor Booker's translation. His notes are a bit of a mess, but Estelle will be able to make sense of them, I hope."

Her eyes rounded. "Was that why Sylvester brought the briefcase in here?"

"He thought it was the safest place to keep the manuscript," I explained. "I don't know why he felt the need to bring that Spell Assistant thing in here as well, but I suppose it'll keep Aunt Candace distracted for a bit."

"Yes..." Her gaze roved over the page. "This is incredibly valuable, even if we don't understand it yet. I'll have to take a closer look at it later when Estelle's back."

"That was what I thought," I said. "She understands how Professor Booker's mind works better than the rest of us do."

"Yes." She placed the manuscript on the desk. "Are the Founders looking for this?"

"If they knew it existed, they would be—but I'm not sure they do," I said. "The vampire attack was faked, which suggests they aren't in the town itself, at the very least."

Evangeline had believed the Founders were in the area, but she'd turned out to be mistaken—a feat I'd never thought possible.

The phone rang, and Aunt Adelaide rose to her feet. "I'll get that."

She crossed the lobby to answer. I scooped up the manuscript in one hand, not wanting it out of my sight, but a moment later, my phone buzzed too. I fished it out of my pocket with my free hand and found a voice message from Estelle.

"Estelle?" I tapped the message, and a buzzing noise answered.

"Rory!" Estelle's voice crackled. "Help—"

She cut off in a scream that set my nerves on end.

"Estelle!" I shouted into the phone, but only static remained on the other side. I called her number and went through to voicemail. "Dammit!"

Xavier took my arm. "Rory—what's wrong?"

I lowered my phone, trembling. "Estelle—she's in trouble, I think. She was screaming."

Aunt Adelaide came running back into view, her eyes wide. "There was an incident at the jail, Edwin said. Something about a breakout."

Jesse. "I think something happened to Estelle. She's in trouble."

Xavier took my arm, steadying me. "We'll find her, Rory. It's okay."

It's not okay. If Jesse had hurt Estelle... He'd already been willing to kill once, and I had the horrible feeling he'd targeted Estelle so he could ensure we did exactly what he wanted us to.

14

Xavier and I left the library and sprinted across the square towards the seafront. Panic blared in my mind, mingling with confusion. Hadn't Jesse been ensconced in a holding cell? How did he manage to escape?

My questions came to an abrupt stop when I spied the giant hole in the police station's wall. Several trolls had gathered outside, and smoke seeped out of the hole, making me cough.

I doubled over as we walked past the gaping hole in the wall, my eyes watering. "What *is* that?"

"Jesse." Xavier held my arm, steadying my balance. "He must have smuggled some kind of explosive into the prison."

"Something he got from the lab, I'm guessing." I coughed again. The area smelled like burnt flowers, and smoke obscured the inside of the police station.

We reached the front as a dazed-looking Edwin came staggering out of the lobby through the automatic doors.

"Edwin," I called to him. "Edwin—where's Estelle?"

"Back already?" He peered at Xavier and me, his face

smudged with a substance that looked like a mixture between mud and glue. "Someone blew a hole in my wall."

"Jesse, I assume." I looked to the trolls for confirmation, but they looked even more baffled than they usually did. "He took Estelle. Did you see him?"

"No." He broke into a coughing fit, sinking to the ground. "I can't see anything."

The doors slid open, and Xavier strode through them. I hastened to catch up to him, but smoke billowed into the lobby, making it hard to catch my breath.

"Rory—stay back," Xavier said. "I don't have to breathe, remember? I'll look for him."

I halted and crouched down beside Edwin. "Didn't you search Jesse when you brought him in?"

"What?" He stopped coughing. "Yes, of course. He wasn't carrying any weapons, and I confiscated his wand."

"I guess a magical explosive would be easier to hide." Jesse was nothing if not resourceful. I'd give him that. "He wants the briefcase back… and he has Estelle. Possibly as a hostage."

I stared into the police station's lobby, my heart thumping, until Xavier emerged with a shaken Professor Colt behind him.

"He was hiding under a desk," Xavier explained. "Rory, are you okay?"

"No, but Estelle's worse off than I am." I leaned over to speak to the professor, who'd sunk to the ground next to Edwin. "Professor—did *you* see where Jesse went?"

"No," he coughed. "I couldn't see a thing in there."

"He took Estelle."

"Oh." His face fell. "That's unfortunate."

"Is that all you have to say?" Disbelief and anger rose inside me. "I found Professor Booker's notes and the manuscript in Jesse's briefcase. Did you know Jesse stole them?"

He lifted his head. "No—you found the manuscript? Really?"

"Yes, but I can't make sense out of the professor's notes." I surveyed him. "Did he successfully make the poison himself? Do you know?"

"No—I don't know." More coughing. "I can look at the notes myself."

"Not if Jesse wants them in exchange for letting Estelle go." I wasn't sure he would—he might just want the briefcase —but given the valuable nature of the manuscript, I doubted it'd slip his notice.

The remaining colour drained from the professor's face. "No. You can't give it to him."

"I can't let him hurt my cousin either." My voice trembled a little, but something inside me had turned as cold as steel, fuelled by my anger at him *and* Professor Booker for keeping secrets that had caused my family to be targeted. "You're partly responsible for this. I'd appreciate your help."

"I… don't know what I can do." His shoulders slumped. "Is the manuscript still at the library?"

"Yes, and I'm not giving it to you either," I declared. "With that being said, I'd appreciate it if you tell me why Jesse was interested in it. He didn't have a shiny academic record, did he?"

"No… no, but Charles wanted to borrow that Spell Assistant of his," Professor Colt said. "I warned him it might be dangerous, but he insisted that it was the only way to translate the manuscript."

"Did Jesse know that?" I asked.

"No," he said, "but Charles claimed that Jesse didn't know how to use the Spell Assistant correctly and offered to teach him, which is to be expected when someone like him is given a spell as complex and rare as that one."

"You think the Founders gave it to him?" Incredulity

seeped into my voice. "Why would they give a rare and complex spell to a cheat who wanted to use it to make money off his fellow students?"

"I… really can't say." He dropped his gaze. "I don't agree with Charles's decision, either, but he didn't deserve to die. He was trying to save lives."

"What did he plan to *do* with the potion?" I enquired. "Assuming he succeeded in replicating the recipe, what was the plan?"

"He never told me." Professor Colt rose shakily to his feet. "But I'm sure he wouldn't have wanted that manuscript to fall into the wrong hands."

Xavier stepped into the professor's path. "Where are you going? I thought you intended to hand yourself in."

"The jail isn't secure," he said. "I'm not going to sit in there and wait for them to find me."

"Then…" I thought for a moment, then I made up my mind. "Come with us to the library."

Xavier gave me a worried frown. "Are you sure, Rory?"

"No, but I'd rather keep him where we can watch him," I whispered back. "We just need to convince Edwin…"

The elf policeman lifted his head weakly. "Are you taking my prisoner away?"

"There's a hole in the wall," Xavier reminded him. "It's not secure in the jail, but the library is, and we'll keep an eye on him while he's there."

Edwin opened his mouth as if to argue, then he exhaled in a sigh. "Fine, take him—on the condition that you return him to me as soon as I fix the damage here."

"Deal." I was less than enthused about taking the professor to the library, especially since Estelle needed our help as quickly as possible, but we had to get backup first. Particularly if Jesse wasn't alone.

"If it turns out the Founders are with Jesse," I said, "what're the odds that Evangeline will offer help?"

"Low," Xavier replied. "Especially if Dr Hayes is still in the church."

I'd momentarily forgotten Dr Hayes, but if you asked me, she'd be safer with Evangeline than elsewhere. Granted, Jesse wasn't in town, and if he hadn't left any trail behind him to follow, I'd have to rely on Xavier's Reaper skills to find him. *So be it.*

"If there's anything else you haven't told us, now would be a spectacular time," I told Professor Colt. "What made Professor Booker think he was the right person to translate the manuscript in the first place? Why not come to the library?"

"I... I can't speak to his motives, but I, for one, didn't want to attract more unwanted attention to the library," Professor Colt said haltingly. "After what happened with your father's book..."

My heart jolted. "You know the book ended up in the library anyway, don't you?"

"Yes, but this one... It's different," he said. "The Founders prefer to keep a close grip on anything that might prove a threat to their immortality, and they would never let that information into human hands. Charles told me the book that your father gave me for safekeeping was less dangerous, though no less coveted."

"What?" I asked in a sharper voice than I intended. "Did you seriously loan Professor Booker the book? I thought you were scared to even look at it."

"Charles was braver than I." He swallowed, not meeting my eyes. "He knew the danger the Founders pose to academics who refuse to bow to their will, but he believed it was worth the risk. He said they have no right to hoard knowledge for themselves."

"Including knowledge of how to kill one of them." Aside from staking and the even less practical method of borrowing a Reaper's scythe, vampires were hard to destroy. "I can understand why they'd want to obliterate all mentions of that poison from existence, but I'm surprised they missed such an obvious one."

"The university has never had reason to catch their attention before."

"Until now." My mind turned over the implications. "What was the plan? Did you want to pick up where the professor left off?"

"I'm not an alchemist," he said. "It was the translation that I could have helped with, but when I realised the nature of the information in that recipe..."

"You backed off and left him to die," Xavier said in cold tones. "Didn't you?"

"No... not at all." The professor shuddered. "I never expected him to succeed in brewing the poison himself, and there are... complications. The poison is always lethal to humans, but if the dose is too low, it puts the vampire into a very deep sleep, one that no common antidote will wake them from."

"Eternal sleep is good enough for Mortimer Vale." A shiver sprang to my arms at the memory of our last encounter. *This is the kind of information my dad was trying to protect. Ways to kill a vampire permanently. Or as permanent as possible for an immortal, anyway.*

The question was why hadn't Professor Booker told Estelle about the manuscript, knowing she and I both lived in the library? If the truth was anywhere, it'd lie in his notes, so we walked Professor Colt into the library.

Aunt Adelaide had returned to the desk, but she wasn't alone. Aunt Candace perched on the edge of the desk, the briefcase lying open at her feet and the box-like spell gleaming within. Cass stood nearby, holding the manuscript. She put it down when she saw me. "Where's Estelle?"

"Jesse took her," I said. "He blew a hole in the prison wall to escape. We brought Professor Colt here until Edwin fixes the damage."

"You're the professor, are you?" Aunt Adelaide narrowed her eyes at him. "You got my daughter kidnapped."

He blanched. "Not me. I don't know why he took Estelle."

"He wants that briefcase back," I told Aunt Candace. "I'm guessing he'd be willing to trade, though he might also want the manuscript and the notes as well."

"These?" Aunt Adelaide picked up Professor Booker's notes, which I'd left on the desk. "I can create a false duplicate easily enough. He won't notice the difference."

"Duplicate?" I echoed. "I guess a manuscript isn't that hard to fake, but what about the spell?"

Aunt Candace nudged the briefcase with her foot. "Don't look at me. My duplication spells can't extend to copying a spell this complex."

"Your niece is *missing,*" I said pointedly. "Kidnapped by a murderer. You're really going to just sit there and translate that riddle while he—?" I couldn't continue.

"No," she said. "I'm going to wait for your Reaper friend to find Estelle's location, and then I'm going to find our slippery little would-be entrepreneur and turn him into an electric eel."

"That's… weirdly specific." Yet surprisingly heartening.

"Do you really want to give him the ability to electrocute people?" Cass raised her brows. "Right, never mind. I'll cast the duplication spell. Give me those."

Aunt Adelaide looked surprised at her for volunteering, but she passed Professor Booker's papers to Cass. "Now… what to do with you?"

Professor Colt flinched under her gaze. "I don't plan to run."

"He doesn't," I supplied, "but I'd put him in a spare room until we have Estelle safely back."

"Gladly." Aunt Adelaide stepped around the desk while Cass pointed her wand at the manuscript.

A flash of light appeared, and the number of papers on the desk doubled. Cass picked up the new ones and surveyed them. "That'll do."

"Yes—for Jesse, not the Founders." Aunt Adelaide's mouth pulled taut in anger that I'd rarely seen on her face before. It reminded me of my dad on the rare occasions that he lost his temper. The expression was odd to see on someone usually so calm and dependable. "They won't easily be fooled."

"With luck, we'll get there before they show up." I eyed the briefcase at Aunt Candace's feet. "I'm not sure any of us can create a convincing copy of that thing."

"He's not getting this back," Aunt Candace said. "I'm almost done."

"Seriously?" I glared at her. "And here I thought Estelle was more important than translating whatever Grandma wrote on that door."

"Your grandmother wrote something on a door?" asked Professor Colt hesitantly.

"None of your business," Cass broke in.

"Is—is it the fourth floor?" he asked.

"I told you, it's none of your—"

"Your father told me about it," Professor Colt interrupted, speaking fast. "He said the fourth floor's protections were advanced enough to require an equally advanced spell to break—but that the only one he knew of was stolen."

"Huh?" My curiosity rose despite myself. "Stolen? What was stolen?"

"That Spell Assistant." Cass's attention snapped over to the briefcase. "It never belonged to the Founders."

"Then—my dad." Disbelief washed over me. "The spell was *his?"*

"Our mother's," Aunt Candace corrected without looking up. "Originally. I'd have thought one of you would have guessed sooner."

"That was why Sylvester brought it into the library." The spell was my grandmother's? But if the Founders had stolen the spell from my family, and it had ended up in Jesse's hands… it all but proved his allegiance with them.

We needed to get Estelle back. Now.

"Of course." Cass swore. "Fine. We'll take the empty briefcase. That ought to stall them for a bit."

"By 'we,' you mean all of us?" I turned to Xavier, my nerves buzzing. "Can you take all of us with you at once?"

"If Estelle is somewhere I haven't been before, I run the risk of losing some of you on the way," he said. "I'm better off taking one of you at a time. Two at most."

"We can use a finding spell," Cass said. "They won't be that far out of range."

"I'll go with Xavier." I had my Biblio-Witch Inventory, my wand, and all the knowledge from the past few weeks and months of learning to fight off vampires. That ought to be enough to take on one disgruntled former student—as long as he hadn't already called the Founders to his side. "He can't have gone far from Ivory Beach, not if he wants us to find him to make the trade."

"You're going alone?" Worry clouded Aunt Adelaide's eyes. "Take Sylvester… or Jet."

"Xavier can't take non-humans with him through the afterworld," I reminded her. "But they can fly ahead and look for us. Right, Jet?"

"Here, partner!" Jet came swooping down onto the desk,

his eyes wide and anxious. "You're not going to fight the vampires, are you?"

"I hope not," I told my familiar. "I might need backup, though. Can you fly around the area and look for Estelle—and if you find her location, can you bring word back to the others? That ought to make it easier for them to find her." I could technically use a tracking spell myself—I'd done it before—but my nerves were on edge, and if Estelle turned out to be farther than my range, I might guarantee ending up lost en route. Xavier was steadier than I was, and his Reaper talents would enable us to reach Estelle in a heartbeat.

"Yes, partner!" Jet took flight. A pang hit my chest. I didn't want to leave him behind, but my familiar wouldn't be a fan of jumping through the afterworld. I wasn't overly keen on the idea, either, come to that—but for Estelle's sake, I'd do it.

Xavier took my arm, and the cold rush of the afterworld swept over me a moment before darkness closed in.

An instant later, my feet touched down on damp sand. As I'd hoped, Jesse hadn't gone far from Ivory Beach, though I didn't recognise this particular strip of sand. Waves lapped against the shore ahead of us, and dunes stretched in all directions.

Jesse was there, a lone figure atop a dune. It took a moment for me to spot an unconscious-looking Estelle at his feet, and his smirk made my hands curl into fists.

"Good, you came." He pointed at the briefcase in my hands. "Give that to me, and I'll give your cousin back."

15

Jesse watched my approach expectantly. The briefcase swung from my hands, empty except for the papers that Cass had duplicated for me. The instant he looked inside, the game would be over, but he was no vampire, and he couldn't read my thoughts. All that mattered was that I got Estelle away from him before the Founders showed up. He had his wand out, pointing it at her limp body.

"What did you do to her?" I clenched my sweaty hand over the briefcase handle, trying to walk as if it weighed as much as it normally did. "If she's hurt—"

"I just knocked her out," he said. "Nobody else has to die."

"Why kill Professor Booker in the first place?" If I kept his attention on me, Xavier might be able to get Estelle out of Jesse's reach before he realised the briefcase was empty. "You helped him, didn't you?"

"And he repaid me by kicking me out."

"For cheating. Which you did do." My heartbeat thudded in my fingertips as he reached out to take the briefcase from me. "I'm just trying to understand why. Didn't you loan him your Spell Assistant?"

"He didn't give me a choice." He snatched the briefcase out of my grip. "Once he found out I had the spell, he wouldn't leave me alone. He wanted it for himself."

Except it's not yours. It's my family's. I held back the words, not daring to say anything that might cause him to focus on Estelle again. Out of the corner of my eye, I saw Xavier appear beside my cousin's unconscious form.

"I'm surprised you were allowed to take it." I indicated the briefcase, now clutched in his hand. "The Founders don't like to share, I thought."

"You thought right." A smirk flitted across his face. "They underestimated me."

"You stole it." Was there anything he *hadn't* stolen? "Why?"

He shrugged. "It looked valuable, and the pendant they gave me stopped them from sensing I was nearby when I took it."

"It belonged to my family." My heart lurched when he lifted the briefcase and frowned as if he'd realised it was lighter than it should be. "That was why Sylvester took it back."

"Yeah, right." He put down the briefcase and began fiddling with the clasps. "Maybe your family stole it too."

Any second now. I caught Xavier's eye, and he lifted Estelle into his arms.

When I returned my attention to Jesse, he whipped around, eyes narrowing. "You cheated."

"As if you wouldn't have done the same." I reached for my wand, but Jesse moved first. After a loud bang and a flash of light, smoke billowed out across my vision. *That wasn't a spell.*

My knees hit the sand as my strength gave out abruptly. What had he hit me with—some kind of paralysing potion?

Whatever it was, I couldn't even lift my head to see if Xavier and Estelle had made it out of harm's way.

"Rory!" I heard Xavier shout my name, but Jesse stood between us. His wand was in his hand, pointing directly at my face.

"Don't come any closer, Reaper," he warned.

Instinct screamed at me to move, but my body remained weighted down by the result of whatever alchemical magic Jesse'd used on me. My hands clenched on the ground, fingers drawing desperate furrows into the damp sand. If I could reach my pocket, I'd be able to grab my wand, or the firedust I kept there in case of a vampire attack—but I hadn't the strength to move.

Was I doomed to meet my end at the hands of a human, not a vampire?

"Let her go." Xavier's voice was cold, dangerous. "Now."

"She deceived me and stole my property," he growled. "Someone has to pay for this."

"The spell was the property of her family, not you," Xavier replied. "And that wasn't all you stole, was it?"

"No," a soft, elegant voice said. "No, it wasn't."

Fear gripped me, momentarily overcoming the weakness flooding my veins. I inched my head upward, and my gaze locked on the newcomer. She stood amid the sand dunes, a tall, elegant woman in a flowing dress that rippled gently in the breeze, her hair streaming loose to her shoulders.

The vampire glided down to the briefcase Jesse had abandoned and picked up the papers that stuck out from within. "What's this?"

"I—" Jesse broke off. "Cateline. I was going to steal back the spell from the person who took it from you."

He knows this woman. She could only be a Founder, perhaps the one Evangeline had been looking out for. Sweat beaded on my brow. Yes, Jesse was the target and not me, but that wouldn't last for long when she realised who I was. On the other hand, he must realise that lying to a vampire's face would earn him a one-way ticket to the grave.

"Lies," she said quietly. "You might wear one of our pendants, but that doesn't prevent us from noticing your trickery. I know you stole our property—and you shared that device with a human who meant us harm."

She meant Professor Booker. She must have been watching closely, perhaps reading the minds of other people around Ivory Beach. Evangeline's paranoia hadn't been off the mark after all.

"I was set up," Jesse argued. "I was innocent."

I couldn't help admiring his nerve. The vampire—Cateline—was silent for a tense moment, surveying him.

"You were given an opportunity," she said. "You were offered the chance to join our ranks, and you chose to spurn our offer and steal from us instead. Did you expect to be allowed to escape unscathed?"

"Take it back, then." He jumped to his feet, gesturing at the briefcase. "The Spell Assistant isn't here because *she* stole it from me. You'll have to get it from her."

He pointed directly at me, and the vampire swivelled in my direction. My breathing quickened, my heart racing as if it might escape my chest. This was my worst nightmare come true—to face a vampire while incapacitated, unable to move or run. Despite the firedust in my pocket, my wand, my Biblio-Witch Inventory—they were all out of my reach.

The shifting of shadows reminded me that I wasn't alone. Xavier appeared, blocking the vampire's path.

"Reaper." She looked him up and down. "Why do you come to the defence of a human?"

"Rory is under my protection," he said. "This man here is the one who has wronged you, not her."

He was stretching the truth a little, given my family's history with the Founders—but it didn't matter; no vampire could read *his* thoughts. The two were evenly matched in a fight, unless she'd brought backup. *Dammit, why won't this spell wear off?*

"They're conspiring against me!" Jesse protested. "I never should have gone near that library."

"Library?" The vampire hissed out the word. "*You.* I should have known."

The air fled my lungs. I mentally screamed at my body to move, but as the vampire's attention returned to me, I could only clench my hands. My fingertips carved lines in the sand, scratching helplessly…

Or not. There was one thing I could still do.

My fingers scrabbled at the sand, scratching out the word *stop.* Again, I traced the words over and over.

"I told you to stay away from her." Xavier's words snapped out, a warning, but I focused on my fingers, etching my plea into the sand.

I wasn't in the library. I didn't have my Biblio-Witch Inventory in my hand—but muscle memory and desperation traced the lines my fingers left in their wake, and a glow ignited. I pushed past the weakness and lifted my head to see that the vampire had frozen in her tracks. Her mouth gaped open in surprise, as did Jesse's.

"Rory?" Xavier was in front of me, his hand outstretched. "What—was that you?"

"Yeah." I took his hand, and he helped me stagger to my feet. Abruptly, I fell against him, the burst of energy dissipating. "That won't hold her for long."

I hadn't used an actual writing implement or paper to cast the spell, but I'd won myself time. Cateline's face twitched, warning me that I didn't have long, while the sound of footsteps on sand indicated that we'd lost our other companion.

"Jesse's running away." I inwardly cursed the weakness in my limbs that prevented me from letting go of Xavier. "You—Cateline—doesn't he deserve to answer for stealing from you?"

The vampire hissed, her limbs twitching as she fought to shake off my spell. "You are far more valuable a target. Aurora, is it? I've heard the stories about you... and your family."

"You won't touch her." Xavier's grip on my shoulder was gentle, but his voice was as hard as steel.

I willed my hand to move, to reach into my pocket for my Biblio-Witch Inventory—but before I could budge an inch, Cateline escaped from my spell. She was behind me in a blink, grabbing my arm from behind and pulling me out of Xavier's grip.

"The Hawthorn family." My wrist screamed with pain as she tugged my arm upward, scrutinising my face. "Yes, I see the resemblance."

"Let me go!" I put every ounce of my remaining strength into pulling free of her hold, but I'd never have had a chance of outdoing a vampire's inhuman strength even in usual circumstances. "Jesse's the one who stole from you, and he's getting away."

Shadows shifted on the sand. An instant later, Xavier loomed over the vampire, with the tip of the scythe inches from her skull. "I told you not to touch her."

If I hadn't known Xavier, I'd have been terrified to death. As it was, I still felt a shiver of fear as the darkness shifted around him, hiding his features.

"Fool," Cateline spat. "A younger Reaper like you ought to learn from your elders that you don't want to make enemies of the Founders."

"You haven't been around here recently, have you?"

Xavier's voice echoed from within the darkness. "I'm already with Rory's family. Not the Founders. Let her go."

"Fine." Her grip on my wrist slackened, releasing me. My knees buckled, and as I hit the sand, I forced my fingertips to retrace the word *stop.*

The vampire halted midmotion once again, trapped beneath Xavier's scythe.

"Wait," I croaked. "Don't Reap her soul... We have to take her back to Evangeline."

My wrist ached—either broken or sprained, I was sure—but I had no time to check on the damage. Xavier reluctantly lowered the scythe, some of the darkness around him receding. "Why does she speak as if she knows the Reapers?"

"Rory!" came a shout from the nearby dunes. I forced my head upward at a cry of "Partner!"

My family members ran towards me, led by Jet the crow. Even Estelle was with them; someone must have revived her from whatever Jesse had done to her.

"Good timing." As the vampire moved, Xavier seized her wrists in his hands and held them behind her back with surprising strength. "Anyone want to give me a hand over here?"

"Don't let him get away either!" I pointed a shaking hand at Jesse, who was a distant figure fleeing across the dunes with the empty briefcase swinging from one hand.

"Oh, he won't." Aunt Candace got on his tail in a heartbeat as the others came running to my side.

Cass eyed the vampire, her mouth twisting in distaste. "Should I call my kelpie to take a bite out of her?"

"Not yet," I said. "Give her to Evangeline."

"What did she do to you?" Estelle peered at my face. "Mum—help Rory out. She looks like she's about to faint."

"Jesse used some kind of alchemy," I mumbled. "Not sure what it was, but I can barely stand."

Aunt Adelaide pulled out her wand just as the vampire broke free from the remnants of my spell. Xavier grunted, holding Cateline's arms behind her back, while Estelle and Cass pointed their wands at her.

In a flash, the vampire's body went limp, and she slumped to the sand. A moment later, Aunt Adelaide's wand lit up, and the weakness lifted from my body enough for me to push upright. My wrist still throbbed, but anything was better than feeling as helpless as I had before.

"I'm okay." I rose to my feet as Aunt Adelaide moved to examine my wrist. "It's just sprained, I think."

A thud came from farther up the beach, followed by a triumphant yell that sounded like Aunt Candace. *Ah. I think she caught Jesse.*

"One of you, go and help her," Aunt Adelaide told the others. "Right... hold still, Rory."

In another wave of her wand, the pain in my wrist vanished. I lowered my hand and saw to my surprise that it was Cass who'd offered to run over and help her aunt restrain Jesse. Estelle, looking pale but alert, stood beside Xavier over the unconscious vampire.

"Thanks." I flexed my wrist. "I don't know if there are other vampires hiding in the dunes, but we're close enough to Ivory Beach to make me think she's not alone."

"I quite agree."

The new voice came from within the dunes. Evangeline. I should have guessed she wouldn't be far behind us.

"I think you'll want to take her with you." I indicated the vampire's unconscious form. "I'm guessing she's the vampire you had Laney searching for?"

"Yes—and you're quite right in that she's unlikely to have come alone." The newcomer peered at the vampire's face. "Cateline. How low you've fallen."

I'd figured that she knew her. There were probably few vampires she *didn't* know, considering how long she'd lived.

The question was, did Evangeline know the Founders had once held the property of my family in their home before Jesse had stolen it?

"Did you know Jesse was wearing a pendant when you spoke to him on campus?" I asked. "I thought you read his mind..."

"I didn't." Her teeth flashed as she scowled. "I knew that he was among the likely targets that the Founders would have tried to recruit to join their number, and I suspected he wore a pendant for that reason, but I felt it wasn't worth expending my efforts against an ignorant human."

My brows rose. "You nearly skewered Professor Colt, though."

Another flash of teeth. "That man is not ignorant, and he committed a personal slight against me."

Okay... "Jesse committed murder. Which I'm sure you guessed. But you didn't do anything..." Because she'd wanted to keep him within sight until he drew the Founders' attention and gave her the chance to swoop in and vanquish them herself.

"He was of no danger to your family, Aurora," she said. "You saw for yourself that the library was not undefended."

Vampires. "He might have attacked other people, you know. Besides, he stole my family's property. Did you know the Founders were holding my grandmother's spell in their home?"

"The contents of that briefcase?" She surveyed the struggling Jesse as Aunt Candace and Cass dragged him across the sand. "Really, Aurora, I cannot be expected to keep track of everything the Founders cheat and steal to lay their hands on."

My hands clenched in annoyance. At least she hadn't tried to convince me to give *her* the Spell Assistant, but expecting a straight answer from a vampire was like expecting Aunt Candace to hold a coherent conversation while on a deadline.

Aunt Adelaide indicated the vampire lying at Estelle and Xavier's feet. "Will you be taking her with you?"

"Naturally," Evangeline replied. "Would you like me to take the other one too? He'll have a harder time blowing a hole in *my* prison."

"I don't think Edwin would like that." I watched Jesse's body fall limply to the sand—presumably, Cass or Aunt Candace had got fed up with him trying to escape and cast a spell that knocked him out. "Given that Jesse stole from under the Founders' noses, he might be glad for a jail cell—a sturdier one this time."

"It's your choice, Aurora."

My choice? "In that case, we'll give him to the police, but—if you think this Cateline has any allies, I'd like to know if they have any more of my family's possessions *before* another would-be entrepreneur manages to steal from them."

For an instant, I wondered if I'd gone too far. Then she smiled at me. "I'll keep that in mind… *if* you are as generous as to give me the manuscript Professor Booker was translating. Did you bring it with you?"

Yes... a fake. I didn't want to give her the real one, but would the substitute fool her? She must have guessed that I wouldn't have risked bringing the real manuscript or Professor Booker's notes out of the library, surely.

"We can talk about that one later," I evaded, "when we find out if there are any more Founders trying to get their hands on it. Is the manuscript the reason Cateline came here, or was she just chasing Jesse?"

"I suggest you drop by my house later to talk with her yourself, Aurora."

She's inviting me to the questioning? The vampire had left me with so many other questions that it'd be worth a visit to Evangeline's home to find some answers. For instance, where had Cateline originally come from? How many other vampires were in the area? And just why had she seemed to expect Xavier to be on *her* side?

16

Within half an hour, my family and I were back at the library. While Evangeline escorted Cateline to a prison cell, Aunt Candace subjected Jesse to a thorough examination to make sure he wasn't hiding any more alchemical concoctions in his shoes or up his sleeves.

"This is a violation of privacy!" I heard him yelling at her as the rest of us gathered in the lobby to wait for Edwin and his trolls to show up.

"He's resourceful—I'll give him that," I muttered. "Pity he had to put those skills towards cheating."

"And he accidentally stole our family's property back from the Founders." Cass snorted. "If you ask me, we ought to find out if he swiped anything else of ours too."

"I don't see him getting away with it more than once," I said. "To be honest, it's in his interests not to blow a hole in the jail this time if he doesn't want the Founders to find him."

Now they had yet another reason to target the library—we'd taken back the Spell Assistant—but I had to wonder how and when they'd stolen it from my dad to begin with. Perhaps Cateline would be able to shed some light on the matter when she woke up. Before then, we had to get Jesse out of our hands—and Professor Colt too. We'd found him hiding in the stacks when we'd returned to the library, claiming that he'd thought the Founders would attack while we were gone.

When Edwin's trolls showed up, Aunt Adelaide was only too happy to hand Professor Colt over, and Aunt Candace marched a shaken Jesse out of the back room. He was covered in what looked like slime.

"What did you do to him?" I asked.

She grinned. "He was covered in so many hidden potions and alchemical concoctions that I gave him a bath."

"In slime?"

"It's an effective neutraliser for most alchemy."

Edwin wouldn't be best pleased if Jesse left a trail of slime all over the police station, but at least the responsibility was out of our hands. As the trolls escorted Jesse from the library, Edwin came briefly inside to talk to my aunt.

I was kind of surprised he made no objection to Evangeline's decision to take Cateline into her custody without telling the police first. His response to the news was a weary sigh and nod. "I can trust that if she has any confessions to make, the information will reach me, if pertinent… right, Rory?"

Translation: he wanted *me* to tell him. "Only if Evangeline thinks it's worth sharing, but I don't think Cateline is local. She doesn't know anything about Ivory Beach."

She knew of the library, but that would be more my problem than Edwin's. I figured he'd had enough troublesome prisoners to deal with for now, and by the time the police had taken Jesse and Professor Colt away, Aunt Candace had gone back upstairs to finish unravelling the code Grandma had left on the door.

"I bet it says something like 'Abandon Hope All Ye Who

Enter Here.'" Cass perched on the desk, having declined to follow Aunt Candace back up to the third floor. "Grandma seemed to be in the habit of *not* writing down the important parts. Like how she created that Spell Assistant thing. Mum, did you know it existed?"

"No…" Aunt Adelaide's forehead scrunched up as she thought. "I know she was working on a large number of experiments, but Candace was always more interested in those than I was."

"Figures." Cass drummed her fingers on her knee. "That must be how Aunt Candace learned to make that translation spell for Rory. Grandma taught her some tricks."

"I guess Grandma made the Spell Assistant as an easy way to translate all those codes she kept making up," Estelle said. "She didn't realise we wouldn't have access to the translator spell."

"Because the Founders *stole* it." Cass eyed the manuscript that Aunt Adelaide had placed on the desk. "What're you going to do with that, Mum?"

"I'll put it somewhere secure," she said. "My sister might try brewing the poison herself, but I, for one, wouldn't object to having another weapon to use on the Founders."

Cass made a sceptical noise. "Weapon? Would any of them be foolish enough to drink anything prepared by one of us?"

"Let us dream for a bit, Cass," Estelle said wearily. "Professor Booker thought it was worth translating that manuscript. I don't know that I'd trust Aunt Candace with a deadly poison, though."

"I hope she doesn't go to the jail to ask for Professor Colt's advice on following the recipe," I added. "Poor Edwin has been through enough."

"No kidding." Cass snorted. "At least he doesn't have to

deal with that vampire… or any friends she brought with her."

"You don't think she was alone either." My gaze cast over to Xavier, who hovered near the desk, silent as a ghost. Had the vampire's comment about the Reapers struck him the same way it had me? "I guess she was a different branch of the Founders than the one Mortimer Vale was involved with. She'd heard of the library, but she didn't know everything about us."

She hadn't known I was dating the Reaper, for instance. Xavier smiled when he caught me looking at him, though his expression was strained. "I'm sure Evangeline will be able to get some answers out of her. Did she invite you to the interrogation?"

"Sounded that way." There was Laney to consider, too; she'd slept through the whole thing, but I doubted catching one lone Founder would bring an end to Evangeline's tendency to assign Laney dangerous missions. "I'll wake Laney up."

Despite the library returning to normal, a sense of unease hung over my shoulder like a Reaper's scythe. I couldn't quite put my finger on the source. We'd caught Cateline, and Jesse hadn't got away either. We had the manuscript and the professor's notes for a poison that might challenge even the Founders. Yes, we didn't have any of the poison itself, but Aunt Candace might have the skills to brew it. If she could drag herself away from solving Grandma's riddle.

Which was another issue. My grandmother, my dad, and some of the professors at the university… had all been involved in schemes that had caught the Founders' attention. While I'd hoped this might be over for now—that I might have time to work on my dad's journal and maybe even get a few words in on *my* journal—it was not to be.

It was nearly dusk, so Laney was already awake when I

knocked on her door. She eagerly agreed to come with me to see the vampires, though my family members were less enthused by the idea. I pointed out that we'd be with Xavier, too, but Cass, of all people, offered to come as well.

"We'll be fine," I told her. "I'm not sure Evangeline will even let Xavier into her home. In fact, I'm almost certain she won't."

"Still." Cass eyed Laney, an unreadable expression on her face. "I don't think that Cateline would have left her allies far behind."

"That's Evangeline's concern, and I'm sure she'll have taken precautions." I hadn't intended to sound dismissive, but Cass's expression shuttered at my words, especially when Laney nodded.

My cousin shrugged. "Have it your way."

I spent the journey telling Laney all about our clash with Jesse and the new vampire's appearance.

"I told Evangeline to stop giving you dangerous missions," I added. "Not sure if she took me seriously."

"If that Cateline came alone, it won't be an issue," she said. "But it doesn't sound like she did."

"No." I glanced at Xavier, whose mouth had turned down at the corners. "She's not local. She didn't seem to know anything about how things work here… including the Reapers."

"Huh?" Laney blinked. "What's that mean?"

"She implied… she mentioned the elder Reapers ought to be on the Founders' side," I recalled. "Something along those lines. Was I the only person who heard that?"

"No," Xavier said quietly. "No, I heard it, too, and I don't like to think of what it means."

My unease grew when we reached the church, but I pushed the feeling aside and knocked on the door. I didn't expect Evangeline herself to answer, but she did, with a smile on her lips. "Ah, Aurora, have you come to collect my guest?"

"Have I what?" I said blankly.

She stepped aside, revealing a dazed-looking Dr Hayes. "You… you're that Estelle's sister…"

"Cousin," I corrected. "Evangeline, what do you mean 'collect her'? Can't she find her own way back to campus?"

"Her memory seems somewhat muddled."

Uh-oh. "She needs a doctor. Or someone who can cure whatever the professor did to her."

"What professor?" asked Dr Hayes.

"He's in jail," I said, mostly for Evangeline's benefit. "As is Jesse Rogan."

"I'll take her to the hospital," Xavier offered. "Rory—let me know how it goes with the vampire?"

"Many thanks, Reaper," said the head of the vampires. I wondered if she'd been trying to get rid of him on purpose. "Come on in, both of you."

I held my breath as I walked into the vampires' home. I knew Xavier wouldn't be gone for long. He'd be a blink away, even while I was among the vampires… but why couldn't I shake the sense of impending doom? Yes, the church was creepy, but it was light enough outside that the cold stone walls and the arched ceilings decorated with spiderwebs were less shadowy than they were at night.

"Has this Cateline person told you whereabouts she was staying?" Laney asked Evangeline. "In the area?"

"I don't believe she had a fixed location," she replied. "Their nearest hideout is no longer an option."

Good… but she came from somewhere. "Why was she in the area?" I asked. "Not for the library. She didn't seem to have considered it until she met me."

"She wanted that spell back," Laney guessed. "Or the manuscript. Or both."

"Or she was recruiting students." That was always possible. "Jesse stole from her himself... but it didn't sound like she was *using* the Spell Assistant."

"She didn't need to," said Evangeline, her tone dripping with disdain. "The Founders are fond of displaying their acquisitions. They have countless display cabinets of manuscripts they cannot read and spells none of them can use."

"But where'd they get it to begin with?" I inhaled. "Can I speak to her?"

Evangeline pursed her lips. "You may, but please don't harm her."

"Who, me?" Then I realised she was looking at Laney. Admittedly, my best friend had something of a reputation for staking Founders in the back, but she looked insulted at the comment.

"I won't touch her," she said. "I want Rory to learn the truth, too, you know."

Evangeline led the way down the stone staircase and into the vampires' holding cells. It was icy cold, even more so than in the rest of the church, and my breath fogged the air as we approached the cell in which Cateline stood. I might have felt sorry for her being imprisoned in a medieval-style dungeon if not for the livid expression on her face.

"Your family lives up to their reputations, it seems," she spat at me.

"What does that mean?" I asked. "You've never met my family, have you? Though I'm interested in how you got your hands on my grandmother's property."

She bared her teeth, which were red around the edges. Had she bitten someone? "Now, why would I tell *you* that? Were it not for that Reaper, you'd be dead at my hands."

"The Reaper." More questions cascaded into my mind. "What did you mean when you mentioned elder Reapers? You've met them?"

To my bemusement, she burst out laughing. "Human naivety… never does it cease to amaze me."

"Tell me what that means." I leaned in more closely, only to recoil when Cateline lunged for the bars.

Laney got in her way, seizing Cateline's grasping fingers and pushing them away from my face. Evangeline moved equally fast, pushing Laney aside, and the next thing I knew, Cateline lay flat on her back in the cell.

"Ow!" Laney sucked her fingers. "She clawed me. Someone needs to trim her nails."

"Careful, Aurora," said Evangeline. "You should know better than to get that close to one of our kind, bars or no bars."

"I forgot." Stupid of me, really. "Laney, are you okay?"

"Better than her." She peered down at the vampire. "What's up with her?"

I looked at her too. Cateline lay limply on her back, the red at her fangs even more obvious than before.

With a furious movement, Evangeline pushed the door to the cell open. As I watched, she crouched beside Cateline and lifted her head carefully with a manicured hand. "She's dead."

"What?" My heart missed a beat. "What—how?"

The crimson around Cateline's mouth drew my eyes again. Had she used some kind of poison? I'd thought nothing worked on vampires—except—

"I'll get to the bottom of this." Evangeline spun back to us, her eyes dark with fury. "I'll ask the two of you to leave."

We did so, without argument. My mind reeled, and even Laney hadn't a word to say until we got outside.

"Did the other Founders give her an order to commit suicide if she got caught?" Laney shuddered. "Her thoughts were too confusing to read before she died, but I got the impression someone else gave the order."

"Did you pick up on anything else that she didn't say

aloud?" I drew my arms around my chest, unable to shake the chill even though we were outside the freezing church. "About the Reapers?"

"No—why?"

"I got the feeling she was familiar with them." Not that we'd be able to ask her anything more. "Never mind. We'd better go back to the library."

I texted Xavier on the way since he wasn't back from dropping Dr Hayes off at the hospital yet, and we walked back to the library in silence. Laney was more subdued than I'd ever seen her, and my questions multiplied by the minute.

What information had Cateline been carrying that someone had wanted her to die to protect? She didn't know my family… so how had the Spell Assistant ended up in her possession? When had my grandmother created it? The other details might lie somewhere in my dad's journal, but I needed to get the translation spell back from Aunt Candace before I had a closer look.

Laney and I entered the library, where Estelle and Aunt Adelaide were tidying up as if it were an ordinary evening. Cass had gone, presumably to the third floor, and Aunt Candace was as absent as ever.

"You're back early," Estelle remarked. "Did Evangeline throw you out?"

"No—Cateline died," I told her. "I think she smuggled in some kind of poison."

"Poison doesn't work on vampires." Aunt Adelaide's expression darkened. "Except…"

"Except for Professor Booker's manuscript." Estelle paled. "No way."

"Her mouth went red," I said. "Like blood."

Estelle swore under her breath. "I haven't read all the notes myself, but that sounds exactly like the effect the professor described."

"Then..." Laney faltered. "The Founders knew how to make the poison all along?"

"Impossible." Estelle gripped the desk with one hand, her face chalk white. "From what Professor Colt said, in a low quantity, the potion will only be strong enough to put a vampire into a deep sleep. It's hard to get the dose right."

"Looks like they managed," Laney said in a hushed voice. "And to top it off, we lost our witness."

"Yeah." I saw a light upstairs on the third floor and recalled that we did have one reminder of the vampires... the Spell Assistant, or whatever it had originally been called. "I'm going to get back Aunt Candace's translation spell."

"I'm going to lie down." Laney glided towards the living quarters, while I made for the stairs. Such was my distraction that I tripped headlong over an obstacle sticking up from the floor and landed flat on my face.

"Ow." I lifted my head, my nose throbbing. I'd landed on... a trapdoor? "Wait..."

A sudden suspicion hit me, and I pushed onto my knees, staring down at the trapdoor that concealed the library's oldest guest.

"Rory, are you okay?" Aunt Adelaide approached with her arms full of books. "Oh, it's that trapdoor. Odd. It's usually Sylvester who uses it to prank people."

"The vampire." I climbed to my feet, rubbing my forehead. "Nobody can wake him up. Doesn't that sound like a low dose of that poison?"

Aunt Adelaide surveyed the trapdoor, furrowing her brow. "Unlikely. He's been here for years, and your professor only managed to translate that recipe recently, didn't he?"

"Yeah, but if the Founders already knew how to make it..." Maybe they weren't the only ones. Vampires might sleep like the dead but not for decades at a time. And he'd known my grandmother, who might have known of my dad's contact with the professor…

Thoughts chased one another around my head, refusing to connect. I needed more information first.

"He's been there a long time," said Aunt Adelaide. "My mother never explained his presence here, but given everything else she didn't explain, it's certainly possible."

Goosebumps sprang to my arms. "What does it all mean?"

Was the vampire friend or foe? Come to think of it, I wasn't sure Evangeline knew he was here. If she knew, she'd never mentioned it to any of us.

"I don't know," she said, "but my sister might be able to offer a hand if she can drag her attention away from that door for five minutes."

"I'll ask her." I continued towards the stairs, stepping around the trapdoor this time. It wasn't like we could ask Grandma or even the corridor's guardian, which couldn't communicate in words—but the one person who'd almost certainly share my drive for answers was Aunt Candace.

I found her sitting outside the door to the fourth floor with the Spell Assistant at her feet and Cass watching her intently.

"Hey." I glimpsed movement on the shelves nearby, the shuffle of feathers indicating Sylvester's presence. "Would it interest any of you to know that Cateline—the vampire—is dead?"

"Not especially," said Aunt Candace. "Evangeline killed her, did she?"

"No—she poisoned herself." I gave the box a pointed look. "With something that looked awfully similar to a certain poison."

"Did she, now?" Cass dragged her gaze from the spell and met my eyes. "I'm surprised Evangeline let her."

"I don't think she expected it." I returned my attention to

my aunt. "There's something else you might want to know. Remember the vampire in the basement?"

"Occasionally," said Aunt Candace. "He doesn't do much, does he?"

"No, but he's been in a sleep for decades," I said. "Can you think of any spell that might cause that effect?"

"Spells, no. Potions, yes... though none that would work on a vampire." Aunt Candace paused, and I could almost see the lightbulb go off in her head. "Well, well."

I inclined my own head. "According to what we've found out so far, the dose of the poison has to be exactly right. Otherwise, it just puts the vampire into a very deep sleep rather than killing them."

"Grandma did that too?" Cass blinked in surprise. "Did she mean for the vampire to die?"

"I don't know," I said, "but I have to wonder if the vampire appeared in the basement around the same time as Grandma sealed off the fourth-floor corridor. What was the timing, Aunt Candace?"

"Oh, I haven't a clue." Aunt Candace gave a triumphant whoop as the box opened, and a piece of paper emerged. "Yes... this is it."

"What does it say?" I peered over her shoulder, but she snatched the page out of my reach.

"It says that the key to opening the door is to speak one's heart's desire."

"Come again?"

"Speak one's desire?" She laughed. "It's a riddle. Excellent."

I pressed a hand to my forehead. "We went through all that for *another* riddle?"

"It's a simple-enough one," said Aunt Candace. "My heart's desire is to see behind that door. My mother wanted to test our conviction."

I had my doubts, but I decided not to argue. "Can I have my dad's translation spell back now?"

"Oh, go ahead." She waved a hand at me. "I left it in my research cave."

Of course, she had. "Assuming the door doesn't eat you, Aunt Adelaide has the manuscript downstairs along with the professor's notes."

"I shall peruse them later." She wore a grin that was entirely at odds with the general mood, but that was Aunt Candace for you. "Wish me luck."

"I'll be in my bunker." Cass turned around, heading back to the Magical Creatures Division.

I didn't think it would be as easy for Aunt Candace to get through that door as she seemed to believe, but I wanted to have a look at the professor's notes myself. Firstly, I needed to tell Laney my suspicions. She hadn't had too many of her own encounters with the vampire in the basement, but she'd been as curious about how he'd ended up there as the rest of us.

I walked downstairs and found Estelle tidying the Reading Corner. "Rory," she said, "my mum told me you think the vampire in the basement was dosed with the same poison that Cateline died from… and you know, I bet you're right."

"Aunt Candace thinks so, but she's more interested in solving the new riddle she found when she finally translated that text," I explained.

"Another riddle?" asked Aunt Adelaide, overhearing. "What does it say?"

"That you can get through the door by speaking your heart's desire," I said. "She seemed to think it was a test of conviction."

"Odd." Estelle looked at her mother, but Aunt Adelaide seemed equally puzzled.

"I'll have to think about that one," she said. "What's she done with the Spell Assistant?"

"It's still upstairs, but she said I could take the other translator spell back." I veered towards the living quarters. "I'll be right back."

I entered the living room and did a double take when I saw Laney lying on the sofa. She didn't normally nap at this time, much less downstairs—she hated being stared at. "Laney?"

Laney didn't move. She lay on her back, as still as the grave. My skin prickled, and I reached for her arm. "Laney?"

No response. I gingerly lifted her hand and saw traces of red on her fingers where Cateline had grabbed her.

"Laney!"

My cry brought the others running to my side.

"What's wrong with her?" Estelle clapped her hands to her mouth. "Is that blood?"

"Cateline." My knees hit the carpet, a scream building in my throat. "It must have transferred the poison."

"Not all of it." Aunt Adelaide reached out and touched Laney's wrist. "She has a pulse, Rory. She's not dead."

Not dead. Not dead but in such a deep state of unconsciousness that she might as well be. I held Laney's hand, felt the pulse beneath the skin, but she was as still as a stone.

"It didn't work!" Aunt Candace's wail of despair cut through the haze of shock, and she sauntered over to the rest of us. "What're you all doing here?"

"Laney's been poisoned." I spoke through numb lips. "She was grabbed by that vampire before she died, and she had the poison on her fingers."

"It's lucky you didn't touch her yourself, Rory." Estelle put her arm around me, offering comfort. "It'd have almost certainly been fatal on a human."

"I know, but she—" I choked off. "Is there a cure?"

No answer came from any of my family members for a long, tense moment. *Was* there a cure? We had the entirety of Professor Booker's notes here, as far as I knew, and the manuscript itself… but nobody so far had mentioned a way to reverse the process. If Cateline knew of one, she was dead, and so was Professor Booker.

But the Founders knew.

"We'll figure it out, Rory," said Estelle. "Together."

Aunt Adelaide nodded. Even Aunt Candace moved closer, holding the manuscript in her hands. Cass would help, too, I was sure… but would our collective efforts be enough?

Or would I have to appeal to my enemies to save my best friend?

ABOUT THE AUTHOR

Elle Adams lives in the middle of England, where she spends most of her time reading an ever-growing mountain of books, planning her next adventure, or writing. Elle's books are humorous mysteries with a paranormal twist, packed with magical mayhem.

She also writes urban and contemporary fantasy novels as Emma L. Adams.

Visit http://www.elleadamsauthor.com/ to find out more about Elle's books.

Made in the USA
Monee, IL
07 June 2025

19004941R00111